JACKSON HEIGHTS

CHRONICLES

JACKSON HEIGHTS

CHRONICLES

When Crossing the Border Isn't Enough

Orlando Tobón
Translated by Kristina Cordero

ATRIA BOOKS

New York London Toronto Sydney

ATRIA BOOKS

1230 Avenue of the Americas
New York, NY 10020

Translation by Kristina Cordero

Library of Congress Cataloging-in-Publication Data

Tobón, Orlando.
   [Crónicas de Jackson Heights. English]
   Jackson Heights chronicles : when crossing the border isn't enough /
Orlando Tobón ; translated by Kristina Cordero.
      p.   cm.
   I. Cordero, Kristina, 1971– .   II. Title.
PQ8180.43.O36C7613   2006
863'.7—dc22   2006042913

ISBN-13: 978-0-7432-8658-9
ISBN-10:   0-7432-8658-8

First Atria Books trade paperback edition September 2006

10 9 8 7 6 5 4 3 2 1

ATRIA BOOKS is a trademark of Simon & Schuster, Inc.

Manufactured in the United States of America

For information about special discounts for bulk purchases,
please contact Simon & Schuster Special Sales:
1-800-456-6798 or business@simonandschuster.com.

For my mother, Emma Cárdenas de Tobón, a woman I will always admire for her great commitment and sensitivity to social causes. She was the person who inspired me to continue my efforts in the community.

Contents

Contents

Introduction

It is both a great honor and a great pleasure to introduce you, dear reader, to Orlando Tobón. The book you hold in your hands is based on the four decades he lived in the heart of Jackson Heights, New York. It is there that he is known as the "mayor of Little Colombia." From his tiny, tucked-away travel agency, Don Orlando does far more than make travel arrangements. To step into his office is to join a steady stream of visitors: immigrants from all walks of life, from every country of Central and South America. They turn to him for finding work, getting an apartment, arranging their legal status, and the list goes on.

Yet Orlando Tobón is more than a problem fixer. He is a living symbol of what we mean by "community." He embodies the warmth and kindness that draws people to-gether. While living and working in one of America's most thriving immigrant neighborhoods, Don Orlando has known many seeking to make better lives for themselves. The stories in this volume are not only about what it means to be an immigrant, but of what it means to be an American. This book is fascinating, beautifully rendered, and essential reading for anyone wanting to understand what we mean when we call the United States a "nation of immigrants." These stories are rare gems, and I have little doubt that readers will count themselves lucky to have read them, as lucky as I feel to know a man as graceful and generous as Señor Tobón.

> —Joshua Marston, writer and
> director of *Maria Full of Grace*

JACKSON HEIGHTS

CHRONICLES

1

The Queen of the Mules

It was another one of those hot afternoons in August, when the heat and humidity come together in the form of an unbearable, unwanted layer of film that coats every inch of exposed skin. One of those days when breeze exists only in the imagination. One glance was all it took to see that the tiny, overworked air-conditioning unit was doing the best it could to bring cold air into the packed office, the same cold air that escaped every time the door swung open, allowing one more person, defeated by the hot weather, to come inside.

The constant comings and goings created a dynamic background noise, fueled by the chitchat of accents that reflected a broad spectrum of Latin America: Ecuadorans, Salvadorans, Mexicans, Colombians, and even a Dominican or two. More than a travel agency, the place was like a miniature version of the United Nations. Presiding over the hubbub was a kind-looking man with a gentle, forgiving smile. Sitting behind a desk that seemed designed for someone far less voluminous than he, Fernando Padrón maintained order among the twenty some-odd people talking among themselves. They spoke of their trials and tribulations as they waited for their turn to meet with him.

The door swung open again, and suddenly twenty pairs of eyes turned to stare up at the tall, slightly gawky young man with the pale skin and apologetic manners. He wore khaki Bermuda shorts and a white cotton shirt that clung to his skin, damp with perspiration, and from his shoulder hung an old leather backpack, as worn out as the sandals on his feet, the kind hippies used to wear in the sixties. He looked left and right, nodded his head to one and all, and, without a word or a flinch, headed straight for the desk.

As they gazed on in silence, the people in the office could tell, more or less, that the recent arrival was not a resident of Jackson Heights. He was definitely a lost gringo. A few of them began to guess about his identity while the young man advanced toward the desk, blissfully unaware that everyone in the jumbled crowd of men and women knew exactly where they stood in the haphazard line of people waiting to see the man behind the desk. One by one, the onlookers called out irritated remarks as he walked past them: after all, they had been waiting around for hours and this guy acted as if they didn't even exist. Sensing that the comments might escalate into a collective riot if he didn't intervene, Fernando stepped in. He was an expert in calming the agitated spirits of his clientele.

Leaning forward in his swivel chair, speaking in an English that conjured up an image of Colombian coffee fields in full bloom, he asked the American, "Do you need help?" And then he smiled.

By now the American had made it to the desk, and in his very broken Spanish, said, "I've come here because I need to ask for your help. I'm a film student, you see, and I want to make a movie about mules."

The mention of this tragic word prompted more than a few fidgets among several of the women sitting close to Fernando's desk. They couldn't have rehearsed it any better: as the American uttered the word, they all bolted up in unison, pressing their backs straight against their chairs, as if waiting for something to happen.

The American's comment made Fernando feel slightly uncomfortable, too, and to keep the conversation from becoming public knowledge, he gestured to the young man, inviting him to sit down in the seat just recently vacated by a man for whom Fernando, with a flourish on his telephone keypad, had just secured a graveyard-shift job at a Uruguayan bakery in Corona to help him pay for the child he recently learned he had fathered.

Slightly flustered by his good luck, the young man sat down and leaned over the desk with his back hunched over, in an effort to create a slightly more private space for their conversation. All the whispers in the room suddenly came to a grinding halt, and he became acutely aware that the people around him were concentrating very hard on their conversation, trying to figure out the nature of his visit. Cocking his head to the side, Fernando leaned forward, transforming his everyday work space into a kind of makeshift confessional.

Before either of them could say anything, Fernando couldn't help thinking, *Another one*. Every now and then he received visits like this, from young filmmakers interested in documenting the plight of the Colombians who arrived in New York as lethal suitcases, those who lost their lives when a capsule of cocaine exploded in their intestines. Invariably, however, the filmmakers were a flighty bunch who eventually disappeared along with their fanciful illusions of Oscar-winning films. Their interest in the Latin American immigrant drama always seemed to vanish as rapidly as it appeared.

"What do you know about mules?" Fernando asked the American kid, who smiled anxiously.

"A Colombian guy in my neighborhood, a friend of mine, told me that his girlfriend worked as a mule, and I think it's an incredible story. I want to make a movie about how they make the trip from Colombia to Queens," answered the gringo, in his almost passable Spanish.

"So why did you come here, to my office?"

"Because everyone tells me you're the mayor of Jackson Heights. Everyone in the neighborhood says you help mules, whether they're dead or alive," he said, his voice too high-pitched to go unnoticed by the other people in the office.

"Well . . . what can I do for you, then?" Fernando asked, sighing.

"I wouldn't need to ask you for much, really. I just want permission to come here to your office and watch you in

4

action. I know what an important figure you are in Jackson Heights, and I think you could be a main character in the story. So all I ask, really, is your permission to hang around here, observe, and take notes."

Fernando was well aware that once someone sat down in that chair at the other side of his desk, there was no way he could refuse a request. He had known this for a long, long time now. There was no favor he wouldn't grant, no problem that he wouldn't at least help to resolve. And this young man seemed like a nice kid; Fernando felt it right from the start. And anyway, he liked the idea of helping someone make a film that would tell a story that he knew so well.

Fernando had always felt that it was important for people beyond the confines of their little neighborhood to hear about his compatriots and the hardships they endured. He wanted the whole country to know about it. But he also knew that it had to be told in a way that would reach the great American public. A movie, even one made by a student, sounded like something that could do that. With this in mind, Fernando told the young man—Matt Schneider—what everyone in Jackson Heights already knew: the cocaine so casually sniffed in luxurious corporate bathrooms and between cocktails at glittering SoHo lounges had reached them via the warm belly of a terrified mule.

The cases that arrived at Fernando's desk were always those of the losers, the people who ended up lifeless, cold, and disemboweled.

"Once," he confided to Matt, who listened attentively, not sure whether to whip out his reporter's notebook or to entrust the conversation to memory, "once, you know, I met a winner. One of the mules who had swallowed the capsules, collected her payment, and started her life over in New York. But you don't find people like that very often; anyone who makes it through something like that has to be real sharp, but they also have to be on the run—forever. If they actually manage to spend the money they've made, they still have to stay on the good side of all the rats hanging out in all the bars, rotisserie chicken joints, and every last corner you can think of in Little Colombia. There's a whole network of them."

With that, he sat back in his swivel chair and took a look around him, making sure that the curious ears wouldn't be able to hear what he whispered next:

"You don't usually hear stories about people who've worked as mules, much less one who's willing to talk." Pausing for a moment, he closed his eyes and whispered, "But Angela, she was different from the rest of them . . ."

Matt said nothing for a few moments. Then he moved in a little closer and murmured in Fernando's ear:

"Angela . . . who's Angela?"

"If you really want to know, come back tomorrow, and I'll tell you more. I have to get back to my day job. . . . These people have been waiting to see me for hours."

Matt returned the following evening, this time waiting patiently until Fernando said good-bye to his last client. After the door closed the two men sat down, face-to-face, and Fernando began to tell the story of the mule who had made it. With a vague, slightly lost look in his eyes, Fernando recalled the story of Angela: the myth and the woman. . . .

Angela Quiñones had made it big, so big that she had become a minor legend in the world of drug traffickers. A kind of Robin Hood of the mules, she was the topic of endless anecdotes that the middle-aged dope pushers told over and over again, though nobody ever really knew what was fact and what was fiction.

She was barely eighteen when she lied about her age to take her first trip. Her new employers, of course, couldn't have cared less about whether she was nine or ninety—as long as she swallowed the shipment in Colombia and defecated it when she was supposed to, here in the United States. Who cared whether she was eighteen or twenty-one? Her new passport would have to be tailor-made anyway.

A life of hard knocks had forced her to become a good deal sharper than most people twice her age. She took advantage of the passport-forging procedure to change her name. God only knows what she must have left behind—a violent home, hunger, abuse—when she invented the new identity with which she would start her new life in New York, made possible by that blessed harvest inside her belly. The old drug pushers loved to regale each other with stories about how she made more trips than any other mule— more than several mules put together, even—in the course of her professional life.

Though none of her twenty-something colleagues believed the stories, the old men all swore up and down that they had met her at least once or twice, and they all talked about how her black eyes glittered with flinty determination. You could see in her face that she was absolutely certain that nobody in this life would ever get the best of her.

Once they almost stopped her at JFK, but a crooked friend at the immigration checkpoint managed to slip her through, just seconds before she would have had to face the dreaded X-ray test.

Unlike the other successful mules, Angela never spent her earnings on drunken sprees and weekend escapades, nor did she ever once dip her nose into the cocaine, wrapped tightly in condoms, that she had swallowed on so many occasions. She just kept on traveling back and forth, hedging her bets against the laws of probability, carrying the poisonous capsules in her expertly silent stomach, and depositing money in the bank for her retirement.

Then one day it happened: one of the condoms exploded. Myth or reality? Who knew? Cojo Cabrera, a retired hit man paid off by one of the local strongmen, and who used to pick the big boss up from school when he was a kid, claimed to have been in the 84th Street apartment the morning Angela arrived to unload her cargo. According to him, her face was greenish, and her forehead was bathed in cold sweat: the unmistakable sign that her life was very much in danger. As soon as she walked in, said Cabrera, she went straight into the bathroom, and when she finally emerged, a long while later, she dangled a broken capsule before his eyes.

Cabrera concluded the story by explaining that Angela always carried a powerful dose of laxative in a little bottle of fruit juice. She knew things could go wrong at any moment, and her ability to react instantly was what had kept her alive during so many years of perilous service.

Exhausted from recounting so many memories, Fernando took a sip of the coffee that he had purchased hours earlier on his way to the office, now ice cold. By way of a farewell, he said, "Let's leave it for another time, okay?"

Matt pleaded with Fernando to allow him back, so that he could see how he dealt with things on a day-to-day basis. Fernando said yes. That was how, for the rest of the summer, the film student religiously turned up at Fernando's office every day.

He would arrive quietly, courteously say hello, and then, failing to understand any of the jokes people cracked, he would head over to a little corner of the office that he quickly made his own, propping his old backpack, filled with pens, slips of paper, his handy notebook, and some book or other, against his chair. A small bottle of water sat next to it.

From this vantage point, he observed everything, capturing the spontaneity of all that was said and done in the detailed notes he scribbled down in his little spiral notebook. The morning an anguished mother appeared in the office, pleading with Fernando to help locate her son who, two days later, would be found dead, Matt averted his gaze so that she wouldn't feel inhibited and so that he could record her tears, her choked-up words, her terror—the "reality moment," as he would later define it over an afternoon beer with his friends from the New York University film school.

With Fernando's help, Matt visited the morgue, interviewed some people at Rikers Island, and talked to the owners of some of the neighborhood funeral homes as well as the vice-consul of Colombia in New York. The vice-consul showed Matt the letters he had received from Colombia, from the distraught families of the poor young men and women who had left home without a word and whom Fernando often sent back, either in a coffin or a little container of ashes, no bigger than a shoebox.

Some nights, after closing up, Fernando would accept Matt's offer to go out for a beer, and he would tell the film student all kinds of stories about the mules, even though he knew the tales would only make him sad and keep him from falling asleep later. But he always ended up talking, quite a lot, because Matt was a charmer, and a very insistent one at that. It was during those conversations that Matt got to the bottom of the mystery that surrounded Angela Quiñones.

Everyone had a lot to say about her, but Fernando was the only one who had heard the words directly from Angela's lips. Only with Fernando did Angela feel comfortable enough to liberate the confessions, memories, and adventures that she had kept locked away in her heart during all her years of silence. She now tried to live a proper life and keep up appearances in the white-bread New Jersey suburb to which she had fled, far from the citizens of Little Colombia who knew her face and her former life too well.

Angela and Fernando met in the middle of the madness of 9/11. The entire city was traumatized, and the Latin-American neighborhoods suffered doubly: in addition to the pain and the shock everyone felt, they were racked with the fear, warranted or not, of potential deportation. Fernando had spent the entire night in his office, filled to overflowing with hysterical people talking nonstop about the terrorist attack, desperate mothers pleading for help finding their missing sons and daughters, and so many others who simply couldn't bear to return to the frightening solitude of their rented rooms.

Early on the morning of September 12, after falling asleep for a short while at his desk, Fernando decided to get organized so that he could effectively help the people who needed him. The television news programs calculated that the death toll might be as high as ten thousand. With his heart racing, he wondered how many would be people he knew: ten, twenty, a hundred? Right away he decided to put out a collection box to raise money so that he could repatriate the remains of whomever came his way.

Just as he emerged from this meditation, which was the first moment of silence he had enjoyed over the past twenty-four hours, he glanced outside and his eyes focused on a slim figure advancing toward him with a decisive step. The woman was no older than fifty, but she was as beautiful as she must have been at twenty: her smooth face, without a trace of makeup, was framed by black hair that highlighted her jet-black eyes, long eyelashes, and regal nose. Fernando was sure he'd never seen her before: an apparition of that sort was unforgettable. She wore a simple, elegant black linen suit and a strand of pearls. A Chanel pocketbook hung from her shoulder. With a straight back and a firm voice, she said, unequivocally:

"You are Fernando Padrón, is that right?"

"At your service," Fernando murmured, gazing at her as if she were a sculpture in a museum.

"My name is Angela Quiñones. I've come to help you in whatever way I can."

Upon hearing her name, Fernando's eyes opened wider

than he would have liked, and he felt as if all those underground stories had come back to slap him in the face. Suddenly he thought of Javicho, the ex-convict he had hired fresh out of Rikers Island, who loved to repeat the extraordinary stories that circulated around the neighborhood about Angela Quiñones. Until that moment, he had never really stopped to wonder whether she was real or if she was just a figment of many people's imaginations, but now he had his answer. The truth was standing in front of him. Angela Quiñones extended her right hand; on one finger an emerald ring gleamed in the light.

From that morning on, for two whole months, Angela worked at Fernando's side, never stopping, never asking for anything, never complaining. They worked together so well that Fernando almost felt as if they had always been a team, and his many years alone, huddled behind that desk, seemed to somehow evaporate. At one point, he even imagined that the sign above his storefront read just ANGELA AND FERNANDO TRAVEL instead of just FERNANDO TRAVEL.

For those two months, she came to his office every day. Sitting next to him in his tiny work space, she made international phone calls, coordinated donations, arranged burials, and contacted the police, the morgue, the hospitals, like a female version of Fernando. The only difference, of course, was that she was the secret source of the money they used to repatriate the remains of the dead; she was the one who paid for the plane tickets to bring, from Ecuador or Colombia, the families of a handful of people who had been severely hurt during the attacks; she was the one who fed the scores of neighborhood volunteers who spent fifteen or eighteen hours a day working in the office.

Her one condition, in exchange for all this, was anonymity. Angela had made Fernando swear that he would never breathe a word to anyone about where the money had come from.

Though they worked side by side for such an intense period of time, with all the chaos and confusion, Fernando never found the time to ask her about herself, about her past, about where all her money came from. He simply never found the time to corroborate whether or not she was the mythical Angela Quiñones.

His intuition and his years of vague acquaintances and brushes with the mafia led him to believe that she was, most definitely, the queen of the mules, and his conviction only grew stronger when he took a moment or two to consider the fortune she clearly possessed. And yet his idealistic heart resisted; a part of him didn't want to believe that this woman he so admired, this woman who had become a kind of heroine for him and for the entire Latin community, had such a turbulent past. After all, he rationalized, Angela Quiñones wasn't such an unusual name, and one would logically assume that the queen of the mules had to be living under a false name by now—that is, if she was anywhere in the area and hadn't moved far away.

One night, around eleven o'clock, they had just finished compiling a list of neighborhood residents who had lost their jobs in downtown Manhattan when Angela sighed, tired from the day's work.

"Oh, Fer, what I wouldn't give for a nice cold drink . . ." Her warm, conspiratorial voice revealed the bond that had formed between them after all they had been through together.

"The bar at Natives must be open," he suggested, and then jokingly added: "Of course, I don't suppose the bars in Queens sound like much to you . . ."

"No, Fer, it's not that . . . It's just that, well, it's been years since I've been to a bar . . . not here, or anywhere, really," she replied, with a twinge of melancholy that made Fernando's heart skip a beat.

"How come?" The question sounded innocent enough, but Fernando's ears, well trained after so many years as an impromptu psychologist, had detected an imminent confession.

"Well, I can't take the risk of getting 'happy' in public, if you know what I mean. God only knows what I'd end up saying, and if I said the wrong thing to the wrong person . . ."

Certain now that he knew exactly what unmentionable "thing" she was talking about, Fernando remained silent. Then, after a moment or two, he suggested they go to the nearest bodega and buy some Coronas. They could drink them in his tiny bachelor apartment and relax a little. He said this humbly, slightly embarrassed, nervous that she would think he was trying to seduce her, but she thought that would be best. They bought the beers and went up to his apartment.

"Oh, you can't imagine how long it's been since I had a beer with a good friend!" she exclaimed, kicking off her high heels and stretching her shapely legs over the table in front of the sofa. Something in her voice revealed a deep gulf of loneliness that tugged at Fernando's heart, for it reminded him of his own lonely life. He himself could hardly remember the last time someone had visited him in his bat cave, that little room and a half that he came home to at night, only to sleep—the same apartment that he fled every morning just after waking up. He didn't even have a coffeepot, because he always preferred to head to the corner bodega, where he could order a coffee and exchange a few words with Mateo, the Dominican who worked behind the counter.

"Where are your friends?" he asked her, as innocently as possible.

"Dead, or in jail, most of them. The rest are still dealing drugs. But I don't see them anymore," she said, knowing that she didn't need to go any further. He nodded sympathetically, leaned toward her, and in the sweetest tone of voice he could muster, said:

"Tell me about it."

With those words he sparked something inside of Angela; it was as if he had activated a hidden trigger. Suddenly, she began talking and didn't stop for hours, laughing out loud many times, and crying even more. At some moments she couldn't seem to find any words at all, and at others it seemed as though she might choke from all the memories that poured forth from her lips.

When they finished all the beer they had bought, Fernando went back down to the bodega for another six-pack, but they got only halfway through this round; Angela didn't need to get drunk, what she needed was a friend to confide in, someone with whom she could unload all the regrets bottled up inside her, someone with whom she could toast, over and over again, like real drunks, to all the things she had left behind: the trips, the capsules, the fear. All those things that belonged to the past.

In addition to confirming some of the more astonishing stories and refuting the more preposterous ones, Angela told Fernando that when she finally decided to retire from the business, she took the hundreds of thousands of dollars she had saved and bought herself a large, beautiful home in New Jersey. In her obsessive determination to never depend on anyone else for survival, she had lived as cheaply as possible, sharing apartments with roommates so she wouldn't have to spend so much money on rent. Eventually she moved to an area where there wasn't a single Colombian for miles and miles, bought herself an SUV, and started a real estate business. Once again she became a moneymaking machine, and from that point on she would never again have to worry about making ends meet.

Her perfect, polite gringo neighbors—manicured lawn, two cars, three freckled, blond children, four dogs—brought her a bottle of Bordeaux as a housewarming present when she moved into her exclusive new neighborhood. She was a successful businesswoman who courteously said hello to one and all in the mornings. A widow with a son at Stanford University, she was reserved but friendly, and said she was from Venezuela if anyone happened to ask. It never occurred to her to change her name; by dint of pure courage she had built the persona of Angela Quiñones, and nobody could take that away from her. At the same time, she didn't care a thing about her well-earned fame in the rings of hell that were the streets of Jackson Heights, a hell she had no intention of visiting ever again, and she felt relatively secure that her past would never catch up with her in the idyllic suburb of Summit, New Jersey.

She also confessed to Fernando, however, that ever

since she had moved away, her life had become both boring and lonely. Fearful that she might be recognized, which could jeopardize all that she had earned and achieved—her respectable life, her tranquil isolation—she cut off all contact with anyone from Colombia and the rest of Latin America. And that was how she had spent the past fifteen years.

As far as romance was concerned, she dated a number of boring men: a conceited Italian, a self-centered man from Switzerland, and a Scottish man whose accent made it impossible to understand half of what he said. After the first date, usually to dinner, the movies, the theater, or the opera, she never felt inspired to see any of them a second time. For practical reasons, she began seeing a colleague, a real estate agent with whom she developed an "adult relationship": seven months of boring sex, little amusement, and conversations that generally revolved around money.

When she said this, Fernando broke out in laughter, and she, not knowing quite how to respond, began laughing as well, and playfully punched him in the arm.

"Oh yeah, and I bet your sex life is a big success, huh?" she said, challenging him with a sly smile, cocking her chin and surveying the surroundings.

His eyes filled with tears, Fernando couldn't help laughing again, and when he was finally able to talk he said, "It seems, my dear Angela, that hunger and necessity have come together here." They laughed together so gleefully that anyone observing them would have thought they were old high school friends who had reunited after thirty years. Two old friends whose lives had taken very different paths, but whose destinies were remarkably similar.

On the morning of 9/11, Angela was so distraught over what had taken place, that the next day she jumped into her SUV and headed for Little Colombia. When she arrived she felt as if she had left the neighborhood the day before; all those years of self-imposed isolation vanished into thin air as she sped down the highway. She needed to help the people who came from the same place she did, to find the family she didn't have, to share her good fortune with others, to seek solace with other Colombians.

"Fernando," she confessed, "these weeks in your office have saved my life."

After a while, Fernando told her about the scores of mules whom he had sent back to Colombia, feetfirst. Angela remained silent for a very long moment.

"I know I'm one of the lucky ones," she said. "But there are more of us than you might think."

Without missing a beat she began naming names of some very well known figures in Jackson Heights who had been her comrades-in-arms long ago: the owner of a fancy restaurant, the editor of one of the neighborhood newspapers, several respected local business owners, the manager of the corner supermarket, even an ex-candidate for city council who had almost won the election. Fernando had heard unconfirmed rumors about some of them, but there were other names that left him speechless.

"You see, not all of us end up with our bellies sewn up like a ball. The herd of mules that survived is not so small after all," she said, with a tight, sad smile.

"I guess it's not something people go around talking about," said Fernando, pensive.

●　　●　　●

One morning toward the end of the summer, Matt reappeared in the office just after Fernando received word that another disemboweled soul had been found dead somewhere: a dark kid with curly hair. He sounded like an exact match to the person described to Fernando in an anguished letter he had received a few weeks earlier.

Matt begged Fernando to take him along to the morgue, and to convince Dr. Murtúa to let him look at the corpse. He did. As they left the cavernous chamber, the innocent gringo looked as though he'd seen the Devil himself. Fernando sensed that this man would never be the same again.

Matt didn't come around for several days after that, but when he finally did appear, he triumphantly announced that he was almost finished with the screenplay.

"Don Fernando, *yo hacerlo muy famoso!* Very famous!" he cried, hugging him euphorically. The following week, when Matt handed him the script with the title page that read "The Queen of the Mules, by Matthew Schneider," Fernando could barely contain his curiosity and quickly began flipping through the manuscript in search of his character. He finally appeared on page 36. At that moment he realized that the real protagonist of the film was his old friend. The heroine, the character all the moviegoers would fall in love with, was based on Angela Quiñones, the one chosen by God, the Devil, and Matt Schneider.

As he absorbed all of this, Fernando felt a pang of nostalgia for Angela. Suddenly feeling very sad, he told the skinny film student that he thought the screenplay was marvelous. Matt said good-bye like a soldier heading off to war. Hugging Fernando one more time, he explained that he was starting classes again—it was his last year before graduating, and he wouldn't be able to come back to the little nest he had created in the corner of Fernando Travel for a long time.

The winter months went by without any sign of life from the young filmmaker, until one morning at the beginning of spring, Matt's lanky figure crossed the threshold of Fernando Travel once again. This time, his presence did not set off a wave of complaints from the people waiting around in the office; by now they all knew perfectly well who he was: Don Fernando's gringo friend.

He was still the same skinny kid, and he still had that vaguely bohemian air, but his appearance had undergone a transformation during his eight-month absence: now he was almost too neat-looking, downright elegant in a sporty kind of way. He wore a pair of sleek, European-rock-star sunglasses, and his mane of hair was now gathered in a little ponytail at the nape of his neck. His sandals, Bermuda shorts, and long hair were gone, replaced by a pair of khakis, a light blue shirt buttoned all the way up, and a cell phone attached to the waistband of his pants, like a perfect young executive. Instead of the dirty leather backpack bearing the flags of Bolivia, Peru, Ecuador, and Colombia that had been used to transport his grimy notebook, water bottle, and green guerrilla hat, he now toted a slender briefcase that hung from a strap slung over his shoulder.

Their reunion was every bit as warm and effusive as their farewell had been so many months before—that is, before he had graduated with honors, before he had received a two-million-dollar contract to make his first film: *The Queen of the Mules*. Matt had come by to thank Fernando for his invaluable help, and also to tell him that shooting would begin very soon. He wanted to film it "right here, on Roosevelt Avenue," right under the clattering, rusty rails of the elevated 7 train. "Local color" was the key phrase with which Matthew Schneider, screenwriter and director, had sold his project to the executives at HWO, the film production company.

"Fernando," he said, "I want you to play yourself; we're going to shoot your part twenty days from now. Here are your lines." With a flourish, he handed Fernando five sheets of paper, protected by a slender, transparent envelope bearing a label that read: "Francisco Rincón, the mayor of Jackson Heights."

The movie shoot turned the neighborhood upside down.

It was the first major movie about Little Colombia that had ever been filmed in the neighborhood, and even though everyone knew it was about drug trafficking, they brushed off the stigma that this fact might otherwise have held for them. They were thrilled to see the story brought to the big screen, dazzled by the lights from the reflectors that hung from the giant crane, and they all fell in love with the spectacular Puerto Rican actress from the Bronx who had been hired to breathe cinematic life into the Queen of the Mules.

For the next twenty days, Fernando seemed disturbed, distracted; he had never acted before in his life, and all he wanted was to play his role as effectively as possible. Every so often, Javicho would run out to buy him a coffee or a pastry from the bakery up the street, to see if he could get his boss to smile, but nothing worked. In his office, there were but two topics of conversation among the ladies waiting on line to see Fernando: the scenes they had watched during the filming that day or the day before, and Fernando's pale face and dark under-eye circles.

What was going on with him? they all gossiped. This was not a physical ailment, they decided, but some kind of bitterness of the soul. He needed to go to that Amazonian Indian, and get him to prescribe one of those herbal infusions with orange blossoms to fortify his spirits; that would perk him up. What they didn't know, however, was that Fernando was suffering from the effect of his visit to the set the day the filming began. Everyone had been unfailingly kind to him, allowing him to walk around and meet the crew. But he had gotten scared: all those lights, all those cameras, all that massive equipment that moved from one place to another. In the middle of it all, he felt small, silly.

The day Fernando's two scenes were scheduled for shooting, the crew came to his apartment at five in the morning to pick him up and take him to his office in a black SUV. By car it took them far longer than it would have taken him just to walk there himself, like he did every morning, but this was their movie. The set designers had spent the entire night in Fernando Travel, and when they finally arrived, Fernando barely recognized his own office.

In order to make room for the voluminous camera and the reflectors that would light up the early-morning air, the crew had moved all the furniture out onto the street, covering it with giant black canvas dropcloths, and they installed a smaller desk where his own desk normally sat.

The worn-out poster of Cisneros that normally hung on the wall—the poster that Fernando had worked so hard to procure twenty years earlier—had been removed because the movie people felt it didn't look "authentic" enough. In its place was a giant poster with a map of Colombia, and the word "Colombia" printed above it in big red letters.

The rest of the day went by in a kind of dream state: Fernando observed everything as if from very far away, almost like an out-of-body experience. All day long the movie people sent him back and forth, to and fro: makeup, microphone test, lunch, shooting, rest, boredom, shooting, and it took all his concentration just to follow the directions issued by the blond woman with headphones, her assistant, a producer, and finally, Matt. The gawky young man who had timidly appeared in his office so long ago was now a real-life movie director who wouldn't stop until he got the precise angle he wanted and the exact take that he had envisioned in his mind's eye. For the one day of his life that he was a movie actor, the only thing Fernando felt was how unbelievably intense and stressful it was to film a movie.

When the crew packed up and the production trucks finally left Jackson Heights, Fernando returned to his everyday life. The project, Matt, and everything outside of his work slipped from his mind. Every so often he saw the movie mentioned in the local newspapers: FILMING COMPLETE ON *THE QUEEN OF THE MULES*, POPULAR LATIN ARTISTS FEATURED ON THE SOUNDTRACK, and so on. But the months went by, and Fernando didn't hear a thing from Matt.

One day he read an article announcing that the film would soon open at a prestigious independent film festival.

On that very same day, someone from the production company called Fernando to let him know that he had been invited to attend the premiere in Los Angeles. At first he wasn't sure, but in the end he bought himself a sober, respectable suit and on the day of his flight he called upon the ever-obliging Javicho to drive him to La Guardia Airport.

On the night of the premiere, he felt like a fish out of water, but he was secretly thrilled to be able to pose for photos along with the famous Puerto Rican actress and all the other actors. Relaxed and smiling, dressed in a tuxedo, Matt greeted him like an old friend.

"I'm so glad you could make it," he said.

Through the newspapers, Fernando followed the film's incredible success. Then, one day, out of the blue, he received a large package from the production company. Inside was a bronze plaque in recognition of his contribution to the film's box-office triumph, and a check for ten thousand dollars. He was truly content: this was proof that the story of the mules, such a complicated story, had managed to make its mark on a larger market and audience.

When it was all over, Fernando returned, as he always did, to his daily activities, seated behind his big desk, resolving the problems of his compatriots in Jackson Heights.

2
The Inseparable Ones

The icy chill inside the morgue of Jamaica Hospital, in Queens, contrasted starkly with the balmy April morning outside. The cold air penetrated his clothes, seeped into his skin, and rushed through the blood in his veins. Suddenly, he felt transported back in time to his school days, and he could almost hear Benja reading T. S. Eliot's poem *The Waste Land*, which began, "April is the cruellest month." How very true.

It had been a long time since he had felt this kind of frustration. Unlike the great American poet, Fernando did not find literary allusions capable of making the cruelty of the world seem noble; all he had was his own rather fragile form of human intervention. At moments like these he could feel his body crumple and his resolve falter as he wondered whether he had the inner strength to confront such things. As he looked down at the pallid face of the young man in front of him, the only way he knew how to deal with the anguish that consumed him was to scream out loud:

"Look what you've done, you idiot kid, you sonofabitch! I bet you thought you were real clever, real brave, huh? Well, just take a look at yourself now, so young and so perfect, getting involved in this kind of shit . . . and now what? How can you come to me like this, for the love of God?"

He was overwhelmed by the impotence he felt, by not being able to prevent this tragedy. He had arrived too late to avoid what had led him to this icy chamber, standing before this defenseless creature. How on earth was he going to face this man's good mother, who from far, far away had believed that Fernando would be able to swoop down in time to save her son? Day in and day out dozens of crises found their way to him, and Don Fernando responded to each and every one of them with a flurry of phone calls, seeking out the assistance of everyone from politicians to workingmen, millionaires to day laborers—anyone who owed him a favor or who just wanted to help those in need. That was how he handled these problems, and more often than not he managed to solve them some way or another, but this time his resources had failed him, and the reality was doubly painful.

•　　•　　•

None of the people present imagined that there was any relationship between the motionless adolescent and the grief-stricken individual who badgered him with anguished reproaches laced with bitter tenderness.

"What kind of story am I going to make up for your mother? Tell me. Are you listening to me? Look me in the eye, look at who's talking to you, you little shit, don't play dumb with me now. Do you hear me? You tell me, I want you to tell me, what's your solution to this one?"

That was what it was all about: a solution. And that was why he was at his wit's end: he was simply exhausted by his own need to solve all the problems that came his way. But all the other problems he'd solved were nothing compared to what he was looking at right now. This sickly pale creature lying in front of him with the dirty, disheveled hair was an angel, a hopelessly fallen angel, that's what he was. Without thinking, Fernando leaned down and took the boy's frozen face in his hands; as he did this the smell of formaldehyde wafted up through his nasal passages, transporting him back to his own adolescence. The young man lying prostrate on the cold marble slab suddenly became Benja, his teenage confidant, the bosom buddy who had been his companion in so many teenage adventures.

The inseparable ones. That's how they were known in the town where they were born and raised. As children, they galloped together through the splendid green fields of Cisneros's massive coffee plantation, and as adolescents they swore eternal friendship in a blood bond, the kind that recalled the ancient pacts sealed by age-old tribal rites by people like the Druids, the Celts, Chinese, Africans. Their bond was just like those of the famous warriors, the mythical Celtic fighter Cúchulainn and his confidant Ferdiad: stories that live on, stoking the fires of the Irish spirit.

Even though they were as different as fire and water, they traveled as a team in the town that saw them grow up. Benjamín, who people called Benja, Beni, Min, and Jamín, was a good-looking kid with dark skin, tiny eyes, long legs, the hands of a bricklayer or a plumber, and a rowdy, mischievous streak. Even when he knew he didn't have a chance at beating someone, he would still put up a fight, because the most important thing for him was to show the other guy what he was made of. He was a real ladies' man—once, he had three girlfriends at the same time—and everyone said that he knew how to kiss a girl better than anyone in the world. He was a rebel, a dancer, an adventurer, a liar (out of fun, rather than spite), discombobulated, lazy, and terrible at everything in school except for Spanish. That was the one subject he actually excelled at, because if there was one thing that always came easily to him, it was words.

Fernando, on the other hand, who was known as Nano, Ferni, Fer, and Nandito, was pale and homely. He had big eyes, and the long hands of a pianist or a surgeon, and he was pudgy and bowlegged, a person for whom silence was the best argument of all. Even when Fernando knew he could get the best of someone, he never put up a fight, because he never felt the need to prove anything to anyone. He was so timid that he'd never had a single girlfriend—

everyone said that he had never kissed a girl in his life. Serene and even-tempered, he had a big appetite for food and for the movies. Most of all he was honest (out of habit, rather than conviction), pious, methodical, conscientious, and good at everything in school except for Spanish, which was the one subject he did not excel at because if there was one thing in this world that was near impossible for him, it was words.

Initially, the Benjamín/Fernando duo amounted to a transaction of mutual convenience, a practical exchange: Nano got Benja up to speed with his homework, letting Benja copy all his exams (with the exception of one), treated him to apple sodas at recess, and paid for his ticket to see the cowboy-and-Indian serials on Sundays. In exchange, Benja taught Nando how to smoke without choking to death, how to dress like a cool rock-and-roller, how to slick his hair back, how to play Ping-Pong and pool, and how to defend himself during the ruthless Friday brawls that, no matter how hard Fernando tried, invariably landed him in the nurse's office, the victim of a kick or a nasty shove that left him dirty, grumpy, and covered with black-and-blue marks.

"I told you a thousand times, man, but you just don't want to get it."

"What don't I want to get?"

"That you can't go around in life being such a good person, because one day they're gonna come around and take advantage of you."

"I don't care. I just don't want to be a bad guy, man. All right?"

"Bad-bad, no, that's fine, I accept that. But a little bad, come on. You have to be a little bad, you have to do something, or else no one's ever going to respect you."

"But that's the easiest thing in the world—anyone, even a pussy like you, can be a sonofabitch if he wants to."

"Oh, knock it off already! You don't understand a goddamn thing! Nobody's telling you to be a sonofabitch, brother, and anyway, you couldn't be a sonofabitch even if you tried. It's just not in you."

"All I want is for people to stay out of my way, and I'll stay out of theirs. Don't you get it?"

"Yeah, well, that's a lot to ask. If it were only that easy, brother, life would be a piece of cake."

"Fighting is a lot more work than not fighting. You should know that better than anyone."

"Yeah, sure. But then you're the one walking around with an ice pack on the bumps and bruises you get 'cause you don't know how to fight."

"But why should I get into a fight with someone? Go fight yourself if you like it so much!"

"Oh, goddammit! There's no talking to you! You know what you do, you make a guy mad cause you're so goddamn good, *marica*!"

For a long time that was how things were between them, looking out for each other unequivocally. They complemented each other perfectly—that is, until the day the earth seemed to swallow Benjamín up. He just disappeared, and for two days that felt like an eternity, Fernando wandered around aimlessly, not knowing what to do or where to go to find his friend. Then the principal of the school, where both boys were in their last year, called Fernando into his office to tell him that his friend had had an accident. Together, they would go to the local hospital to see him. It turned out to be the longest walk he ever took, for what awaited him at the end was Benjamín's dead body. Before it had even started, his friend's life had been taken away with seven bullets that two gunmen fired into his body, just after his eighteenth birthday. After that, for a long time, Fernando refused to accept gifts or celebrate at all, wanting nothing to do with anything that would distract him from the terrible silence into which he retreated. Not long after that, he left Colombia and went far, far away.

Never again would he celebrate his birthday, not even once in the forty years that followed. Never again, he told himself, would he ever look at someone in that same situation, and yet here he was, forty years later, breaking the promise he had made to himself the day the principal had pulled him out of class and brought him to the morgue. Then, as now, he had had to face the lifeless body of a teenager stretched out on a cold, hard slab spattered with blood. They were interchangeable in his mind: Benja, his best friend, and Rafa, the son of Doña Domitila Sarmiento, who had sent him a letter from Medellín with a photograph of her younger son, begging him to look for him because he had disappeared several days earlier.

As he pondered the sight of Rafael Sarmiento, a shiver ran through his body. They were identical: the same devilish eyes, the serene expression across the lips, the messy hair, and the angular cheekbones that looked as if they had been sculpted with a chisel. It couldn't be, but yet, there he was, the spitting image of Benjamín, the confidant with whom he had tasted his first drop of alcohol, his first puff of marijuana, the same boy who had always let him score whenever they played on opposite teams in soccer games, the same boy who had taught him how to dance to folk songs to seduce women; the same one who, on rainy nights, dared him to swim in the turbulent waters of the river without a bathing suit. The best friend he ever had. From that moment on, a feeling of doom came over him, heavy and inescapable.

If things had happened just a bit differently, he might never have found out about Rafael's tragic end. Just as in certain plays, or in those Hitchcock films he loved so much, things had an odd way of coming together. The night before, he had been getting ready to close up after a long day during which he had scarcely moved from his chair, handling the requests of over a hundred people who had come to see him. Some cases were more complicated than others: a cheating husband, for example, who had abandoned his wife and small children, leaving them with no money. In that kind of situation, Fernando would have to rack his brains to think of the right contact or contacts who could help solve the problem with a job, an apartment, a day care center for the children, a bag of groceries with basic provisions. Sometimes, though, the person in front of him simply wanted a bit of advice, imparted with thoughtfulness and wisdom, and for this he trusted his well-honed instincts. Over the years he had become something of an amateur psychologist, and he almost never got it wrong. In any event, that particular evening he was getting ready to leave when Doña Leonor, his third-floor neighbor, suddenly appeared at his doorstep, her face ashen and her eyes red from crying.

Fernando tried to calm her down, but it was impossible. In between sobs she somehow managed to explain the reason for her distress: Juliana, her oldest daughter, normally finished work at seven in the morning, when she would leave the Hotel Marriott on Lexington Avenue, where she worked the night shift as a chambermaid. The last time she had been seen was at seven A.M. that day. Juliana hadn't answered her cell phone or returned home, and nobody in the entire neighborhood had seen her, either: not the Mexican lady at the fruit and enchilada stand, not the old Colombian man who sold *obleas con arequipe* at the bottom of the stairway below the elevated train, whom she passed every day before she turned onto 82nd Street. Nobody. No matter how many errands she had to run that might make her late, Leonor's daughter never, ever returned home after nine A.M. If something came up she always called her mother. She had never disappeared like this before. Something must have happened to her on the way home, Doña Leonor said, desperate.

As he often did whenever bad fortune took a swipe at one of the families in his community, Fernando launched one of his emergency search operations. First he called his many friends at the local radio stations, hospitals, and police stations, and then sent them a fax with a recent photo of the missing girl. As he carried out all of this frenetic activity, Doña Leonor sobbed and sobbed inconsolably, her fingers clutching a rosary. Juliana was her pride and joy: she performed the most backbreaking work in order to earn a living for her family, and religiously sent money back home to help out with the children who had stayed behind in Bogotá. Doña Leonor would never forgive herself if something happened to her daughter. With every passing minute, the uncertainty grew heavier and heavier in her chest.

They were at the end of their proverbial rope when finally, long after midnight, they received the phone call they were dreading: it was an investigator from the NYPD, calling to tell them that the body of a young woman, stabbed in the chest, had been found near the Queensboro Plaza subway station. She was found without identification, but she did seem to match the physical description of the girl Fernando and Doña Leonor were looking for. The investigator murmured to Fernando that the girl showed signs of having been raped, and then he added,

"Someone has to come and identify the body."

As soon as the forensic pathologists removed the turquoise-colored sheet covering her face, Fernando knew that it was Juliana, whose bruised face bore a terrified, shocked expression. *"Virgen santa!"* he exclaimed in a whisper, when he saw that her throat had been slit.

"Poor baby," he whispered, wiping a tear from his cheek. Then he crossed himself and, his head bowed low, placed his arms across his chest as he recited the Our Father. After that, of course, came the endless round of mind-numbing details and exorbitant fees that nobody could afford. Embalming or cremation? Repatriation of remains? Metal or wood coffin? Who could possibly think of such things at moments like these? The paperwork took them into the

early dawn hours while Doña Leonor's family waited outside in the hallway, broken and inconsolable.

"Despite everything, this little girl was lucky, comparatively. At least she has someone to bury her," said Fernando's old friend, Dr. Víctor Murtúa, director of the morgue. "Lots of times nobody comes to claim them at all." Solemnly Murtúa continued on with the work that made most casual observers run retching from the room after watching for only a few moments. Some people fainted on the spot, overwhelmed by the sight of something that is so very difficult to imagine: how very little is left of a poor human being after an autopsy.

"God, it's cold in here!" Don Fernando said, buttoning up his jacket with two hands.

"Yeah, just imagine what it's like to work here in the winter," the forensic pathologist remarked. "No matter how much snow falls, we're the only ones who can't ever turn on the heat."

"God almighty, that sounds awful."

"Not as awful as having to send another Christian to the garbage dump."

"Are there really that many, Doctor?"

"You wouldn't believe how many, Don Fernando."

"And are they always so young?"

"Yes, that's the saddest thing of all, because it really gets you thinking: these kids had two parents who waited for them and dreamed of them, and raised them and dressed them and took care of them, all so that they could end up like this, sixteen or seventeen years old, stretched out, faceup, with their insides ripped to shreds like a piece of fish . . ."

"It really gives you something to think about. And I guess it makes you wonder, 'What if this was my child?'"

"But that's the most unbelievable thing of all. You can't imagine how many sliced-up kids they bring us every day, and you know what, nobody ever knows or cares about it."

"The newspaper reporters don't come around?"

"Oh, please, forget it. They couldn't care less by now. Mules stopped making the news a long time ago."

"There's a lot of them, then, who come here dead, with the drugs in their stomachs?"

"Sometimes I get as many as three a week. By the time they get here, the drug dealers on this end have already cut their stomachs open and taken all the coke out. They do it just as if they were gutting a chicken, and that's it, man. They just throw the bodies anywhere, disemboweled."

"What scum. Is it possible that nobody cares enough to do anything?"

"Listen, it's the same story as the people who die crossing the border. The newspapers don't say one word about them anymore; they've become part of the routine, you know?"

"The worst thing about it is that nothing ever happens to the mafiosos, who just keep on killing more and more of these young kids," Fernando commented drily.

"A little while ago they brought us another one: a little punk who looked like he was barely out of school. It would break your heart, Don Fernando . . ." Dr. Murtúa paused for a moment, pensive. Then he said, "Come with me, I want you to see this."

During his years as the head of the Jamaica Hospital morgue in Queens, and several other morgues as well, old

Dr. Murtúa had been witness to some of the most bizarre tales about how the living assimilate and relate to the dead: stories that involved everything from the miraculous resurrection of cataleptics to the despicable trade of body snatchers. The saddest, maddest experiences known to man had passed before his wise old eyes. Murtúa had seen all different kinds of emotions and reactions to death, from the heartbroken and tender to the deranged and even the gruesome. In this area of life experience, he thought, there was nothing he hadn't seen. Little did he know that when he opened the heavy door and entered the room reserved for the unidentified bodies, he was in for a surprise.

As he laid eyes on the adolescent body of Doña Domitila's son, stretched out on the marble slab, Fernando Padrón, the man everyone turned to when they needed someone to solve their problems, lost control for a moment. For the second time in his life Fernando felt the earth quiver beneath his feet, and he felt that he was touching bottom in a kind of free fall that plunged him into an abyss of complete and utter devastation. Before the dumbfounded eyes of the forensic doctor, all the pain, fear, frustration, impotence, anguish, and solitude inside of Fernando suddenly bubbled up and he began to rebuke the dead body in a loud voice.

Seeing this young man brought back so many memories for Fernando, memories that gripped his neck, squeezing it so tightly that he found it difficult to breathe. The forensic pathologist was startled and moved by what he saw, for it was something he hadn't thought possible anymore, and he quietly observed the almost paternal anguish of the man berating the cadaver lying before them.

"All right, damn it, what the hell am I going to tell that poor woman who's been looking for you like crazy all over Colombia for weeks now? What kind of heartless sonofabitch are you, that you're going to make me destroy your poor mother, who can barely take any more as it is, that's how desperate she is?"

The sobs rose higher and higher until they were throbbing in Fernando's throat. Finally, he cried.

He had no idea how much time he'd been there: maybe minutes, maybe hours. He still wasn't sure as he descended the metal stairs of the elevated train, the same stairs that Juliana had walked down every morning on her way back to the apartment she shared with Doña Leonor. Her feet would never touch those stairs again.

Even before turning onto 82nd Street, he could make out the line of people standing in front of the tiny storefront he rented inside a shopping center on Roosevelt Avenue, a few yards from the subway stop. He turned the corner. Everyone was gossiping, wondering what had made Don Fernando, who was known for his punctuality, arrive so late. At that particular moment the volume of the streetside chitchat competed with the sound of the cars rushing down the street and the number 7 train above, which passed by every five minutes. Fernando Travel, his jampacked office, was directly below the train stop that connected this working-class neighborhood to one of the world's great cities. On that street corner, unknown to the majority of the people who traveled up and down the grand avenues of New York City, Don Fernando was the savior, the man who was able to fix any problem, the man who couldn't get to the bodega on the corner without getting stopped on the way by one person after another, greeting him, thanking him, imploring him for help.

Life went on. He walked down the steep set of stairs, opened the top button on his white shirt, and breathed in the polluted air. Then he bought an *oblea con arequipe al paisa*, and he thought of Juliana. Just as he did every day, he stopped at Mateo's bodega, where he drank a hot *café con leche*. Today, more than ever, he would need it: the day was just getting started and he was already exhausted. The minute he crossed the threshold of Fernando Travel, he would have to face a whole host of new challenges, for it was April 15, tax day. And like every year, the accountant without the CPA after his name would work until midnight preparing the documents of his *paisas,* his people. The fifteenth of April, the cruelest month of the year. But April is also the month that heralds spring, nature's promise of eternal rebirth, a reflection of life's infinite wisdom. And that was precisely how Fernando felt doing good things for people.

3
You Are Here

His mind was made up: he had enlisted in the U.S. Army and volunteered to fight in the Vietnam War, certain that this was the path to achieving the prosperity his family had never enjoyed. Fernando Jeremías Padrón Mendoza, a nineteen-year-old citizen of Colombia, arrived at La Guardia Airport, in New York, at 3:30 P.M. on February 17, 1968, having traveled from Cisneros, the city in the province of Antioquia where he was born and raised.

He had procured the plane ticket that would change his destiny for $164, purchased on credit, to be paid back in twelve monthly payments of $18. He was, however, aided by a fortune that consisted of four $20 bills, evenly distributed among the pants pockets of the only suit he owned; tucked inside a couple of those pockets were also small, card-sized images of the Virgen del Carmen and St. Jude Thaddeus.

The clattering noise produced by the immense, rickety plane in no way dampened the enthusiasm of the crowd traveling, an assortment of crazy kids who had saved up their money for months and months with the sole intention of escaping the place where they would never be able to improve their standard of living. In exchange for this opportunity, they had agreed to enlist in the armed forces of the United States of America, to fight in the Vietnam War; if they returned alive they would obtain U.S. citizenship and veterans' benefits.

Some of the men had been friends since childhood, some of them had only just met, but they all had one thing in common: none of them had ever traveled on an airplane before. The excitement of their first flight, and the sensation that they were all embarking on an adventure that promised them a prosperous future in the United States, only added to the atmosphere of anticipation and glee. Together they told stories and sang songs like "La Pollera Colorá" in high, falsetto voices, as if they were in a bar in any one of their hometowns.

Eight of them were from Cisneros, and when they found each other they formed a little group so that they might take their first steps in the United States as a team: steps that, according to the plans, would take them to the swamps of the Viet Cong. As often happens in these situations, one young man assumed leadership of the little group, and it wasn't Fernando. It was Federico Castaño, one of the older boys, whose stewardship was warranted by the fact that his brother was a paratrooper in the Marines and had been at the front for several months already. Federico's brother's wife had agreed to put them up for a while in her house in Staten Island, though God only knew that none of them had the slightest idea where that was.

The pilot received a warm round of applause for his peerless landing of the plane, which felt like a coffee machine with wings and motors, transporting them from the past to the future without any trouble aside from a bit of turbulence. The future members of the U.S. army battalion known as "Mi Antioquia Querida" filed past the smiling immigration officials who warmly welcomed the foreign recruits who had come to relieve some of the soldiers currently fighting in Southeast Asia.

"Line up. One after the other, behind me," Castaño ordered.

The men—Fernando included—instantly formed a tight, straight line, a human chain that advanced through the airport corridors, each man holding on to the backpack of the man in front of him. They were like a pack of little elephants, clinging to one another's tails. It was important to ensure that they wouldn't get separated and lost forever in that frantic human jungle. They were amid people of every color of the rainbow who seemed to speak all the languages of the world except their own.

They could hardly believe it, but to get to the blessed home of the soldier Castaño, they had to take a bus, then a train, and then a ferryboat. In Colombia, they couldn't think of a single town, not even the remotest, tiniest village, that was so far away you had to take a train and a boat to get there. And even more incredible, the tiny little island was, in fact, inside the confines of the city of New York!

This was, of course, only the first surprise of many. Their mouths fell open in awe when they arrived at Grand Central Terminal to find not one single train there: in New York, they learned, the trains traveled under the ground. Man, oh, man, they said to each other, everything here is from another planet! Like submarines but on land instead of water! They marveled at this for a long while, unable to get over their shock. At some point, a Puerto Rican lady walked them over to a gigantic map of the city that hung from a wall alongside various posters advertising movies, plays, beauty products, newly opened restaurants, a myriad of possibilities. Together, the eight young men studied the train route they were to take.

"You are here," declared a map with a little arrow pointing to the place they were standing at that moment, though none of them had any idea where they really were. Without a word, Castaño, leader of the pack, placed his finger on the map and traced an invisible path down the green line. This represented the train route which, they had been told, would get them to the South Ferry terminal. The ferryboat would take them to the house that Castaño knew so well from the many photos his brother had sent home to Colombia: a house with a little yard where the flag of his brother's new country, the red, white, and blue one, waved in the air.

"Here comes the train, man, move it!" shouted the aforementioned ringleader, and the young recruits broke into a run, but they ran down the wrong staircase and ended up on the opposite platform. Not understanding how to get to the other side, they ran this way and that, until finally they ran back up the stairs, two steps at a time, and went down the staircase that led to the train.

Predictably, the first to cross the threshold was Castaño, huffing and puffing and shouting the whole way through:

"Get in through whichever door you can, fast!" Right behind him was John Valdelomar, ex-goaltender of the school soccer team; the third one on was the rowdy Negro Abarca; then came Jimmy Manrique, the son of the local tailor; fifth, the annoying four-eyed Giusepi Salgato; sixth, the skinny kid with big ears and a sad face, a quiet boy whose name nobody ever remembered because he never opened his mouth; Willington Murrieta was the seventh one to board the train, and he only barely made it on because halfway across the platform his shoe fell off and he had to stop and pick it up and then race on toward the train in a semi-limp. He made it, but he was the last one to squeeze through the doors as they were closing.

They tried, unsuccessfully, to stop the conductor by yelling, as they did in their home country,

"Suben, patrón, suben!"

Panting and completely disheveled, good-hearted Fernando Padrón stood on the platform pleading with the conductor to open the door. At that instant, all the enthusiasm and spirit that had been fueling him ever since he had left Colombia turned into pure despair. Despite the whistles, hoots, kicks, and screams of his companions, the train began to depart the station. As he stood there outside, on the platform, the last thing he saw was Castaño's distorted face, pressed tightly against the window in such a way that Fernando couldn't possibly understand a single one of the instructions his battalion leader was issuing from inside the train. In a matter of seconds the train was gone, leaving behind the most chilling silence. The young man felt deeply, profoundly lost.

"Where the hell am I?" wondered poor Fernandito, which was the nickname his good mother still called him. As his eyes brimmed over with tears, he felt more alone than he had ever felt in all his life; he almost felt if he had been paralyzed. He had no idea what to do. Pray? Run? Cry? A few minutes later, he walked back over to the subway poster and tried to retrace the path Castaño's finger had followed down the subway line of that giant city. Suddenly he felt like a microscopic dot, lost somewhere on that gigantic map, an invisible little dot with a monstrous red arrow pointing somewhere, with the words *You are here*. Words that meant little or nothing to Fernando right then.

All he wanted was to feel the security of his home, his neighborhood, his town, where everything was familiar, where he didn't need a map to find anything, not even the tiniest little corner. He needed all these things because they were what would bring him to his mother, who would wrap her arms around him in a tight, enveloping embrace. He could almost hear his mother's voice saying,

"Things happen for a reason, my son. It's for the best."

At that moment, his mother's words comforted him, just as they always did whenever something in his life didn't turn out as he'd planned, and he repeated the wisdom to himself.

Alone on the train platform, he asked himself why he had decided to leave behind everything he knew to come to this strange place where he didn't even know how to say "good morning"; where he didn't understand a single thing anyone said, and where he could only stammer, with great difficulty, phrases like "thank you" and "please." So soon after arriving, he was already sorry that he had come to America, and as he foundered in a kind of eerie darkness, he rued the day he had decided to leave home.

It was all because he was fat. It was all because of the fat he'd never managed to control. His fat body was the reason he hadn't been able to make the train. His fat body that had always condemned him to finish last in every race, had once again gotten the best of him, in a completely foreign city no less. What could he do? Well, he could either take the next train in the hopes of catching up with his companions, or else he could sit down and wait to see if they came back for him. The latter was the most logical thing to do; everyone knows that when you get lost, the best thing to do is stay put until someone comes to get you. Or maybe not.

Thirty-seven trains went by before Fernando finally admitted to himself that nobody was coming back to get him, that the time had come to take the situation into his own hands and look for someone who spoke Spanish so that he could ask how to get to that goddamn island where Castaño's brother lived. What the hell was that island called? Dejected, he climbed the grimy steps one by one. Using a series of gestures, charades, and ridiculous faces, he intercepted every last person who crossed his path and asked how to get to that island whose name he couldn't remember.

"Coney Island?" a teenage girl asked him.

"Long Island?" inquired an elegant gentleman.

"Fire Island?" replied a tall, skinny kid.

"Roosevelt Island?" asked a woman dressed in gray from head to toe.

It could have been any of them, or none of them.

"I don't know, sir, I don't know, all I know is that it's an island!" he cried in bewilderment to an old Argentinian man with a kindly face who was sitting on a folding chair and playing a *bandoneón*.

"You have to remember the name—if you don't, you're through, kid. An island: you're nuts, kid. An island? I don't know if you know but at this very moment you happen to be on an island."

That was how he found out. At that moment he thought back to his secondary school literature teacher, an Anglophile with metaphysical pretensions who, whenever he had the chance, would repeat that old saying about how "no man is an island," something that Fernando would repeat to himself in the future.

Never in his wildest dreams would he have imagined what lay in store for him when he left the train station. That day, he would come into contact for the very first time with something truly marvelous: snow. Not even the cold that made him shiver like a leaf could spoil the sense of wonder that came over him as he gazed out at the light snowflakes. They descended from the sky in a lovely dance that he would remember for as long as he lived. And then, he felt happy; it was an odd kind of happiness that he'd never known before, and he promised himself that he would do whatever it took to make his way on that island, so filled with contrasts everywhere he looked.

Finally he returned to that massive building, Grand Central Terminal, to seek refuge before he turned into an ice statue. Lucky for him the building had heat. There, inside, he would figure out what path to take to get himself to that island where his friends were. Like a great big puzzle.

He settled down on a bench and curled up, surprised that nobody was shocked to see him do so. He wondered what his mother would think if she ever found out how her son spent his first night in New York. With that sweet presence, he fell asleep, in the shadow of the great clock, while outside the snow fell down upon the city shrouded in silence.

4

A Fund-raising Campaign

Nothing annoyed Dr. Murtúa more than being interrupted with trivial distractions while he was busy at work. For Dr. Murtúa, a man who did not even possess a television set, everything related to entertainment was a waste of time. While concentrating intently on the dead body of the young girl whose throat had been slit in Queens, he suddenly heard a knock on the door.

He glanced up and, as usual, saw no sign of his assistant, who was generally engrossed in a world that revolved around the rhythms of the distasteful apparatus that seemed permanently attached to his ears. Shrugging his shoulders, the doctor tried to ignore his unexpected guest:

he despised this type of unannounced visit. After a few seconds, however, the insistent knocking forced him to abandon his reflections. Grudgingly he walked over to the door. As he opened it, he practically banged right into an attractive redhead standing in front of a camera, the kind of camera used by reporters to nose around in other people's private lives at the least opportune moments. Once the door was open just a crack, the reporter tried to shimmy her way into the sacred precinct of the morgue laboratory. Aghast at this insolent invasion of his privacy, Dr. Murtúa clung to the doorframe and tried to repel the intruders as quickly as possible.

"I'm sorry, miss, but I can't let you in," he said in a courteous voice as his hand flew up to his tortoiseshell eyeglasses with thick lenses.

"I promise you I will not turn on my camera if you don't allow me to," announced Leyla Sonora, the star reporter for Channel 22, one of New York's Spanish-language television stations.

"Well, if you don't want to tape anything, I don't see why you want me to let you in."

"I'm investigating the murder of Juliana Restrepo. I need to ask you some questions."

"Investigating? *Caramba*, good for you! And may I ask to what I owe this miracle?"

"Please, Doctor, don't insult me. In case you didn't know, we are the number one show in investigative reporting on Spanish-language TV."

"Oh, really? You don't say! Since when?"

"Doctor, please! We are just about to celebrate five years on the air."

"Well, I've been in charge of this morgue since way before you were even born, and I know the face of everyone who has ever been killed in this city. On the other hand, this is the first time I have ever laid eyes on you, Miss Investigative Reporter."

"Well, I guess that's because they haven't managed to kill me yet."

"I can do without the black humor, if you don't mind."

The frosty banter went on like that for a little while longer, to no avail for the reporter, who was unable to establish any kind of amiable dialogue with the forensic pathologist until he finally gave up and asked her:

"All right, all right. What exactly do you want to know?"

"I already told you, Doctor. The Restrepo case, the girl who was found dead, with her throat slit at a subway station."

"Get to the point, miss. What's your question?"

"Was Juliana Restrepo related in any way to the drug trafficking business?"

"You aren't taping this, is that right? Turn that camera the other way."

"I gave you my word, Doctor, the camera is turned off."

"You'll have to excuse me, but I don't want to appear on TV, not on your program or on any other one for that matter."

"I promise you, Doctor, this is off the record. Please just answer me, for God's sake!"

"First tell your cameraman that he shouldn't try so hard to act distracted because I just saw the little red light on his camera. I'm not that gullible."

"I have given you my word that I will not include it in the segment, and I won't."

"And I give you my word that if my face appears on your show for even half a second, I will sue your station so fast that in order to pay me they're going to have to turn me into a shareholder of the station. Understood?"

"Understood, Dr. Murtúa, understood."

"You've been forewarned, then. Fine."

"All right. Will you answer the question now?"

"Pleased. What was the question again?"

Don Fernando arrived at his office, ready to solve the needs of the loud, grumbling multitudes who had been standing on line all morning to see him. Most of them were there seeking help filling out their much-dreaded tax forms, a service he provided for a very nominal fee. He settled in, but no matter how much he tried to concentrate on his work, he simply couldn't stop thinking, not even for a minute, about the dead people with whom he had started out the day.

He was thinking of the two of them, for the sight of the skinny young boy and poor Juliana had been equally shocking. There were moments when he actually thought he could see her walking past the window of his office, her hair pulled back in a braid, dressed in her tight hotel uniform, and her springy gait, just like that of a young gazelle.

His mind then drifted to the two mothers, shattered by their loss, inconsolable. Both came from hardworking families that would never be able to pay the funeral costs. They would never be able to put together the eight thousand pesos that were required in New York for the most austere burial, not even if they had a year to do it. He was going to have to send Rafael Sarmiento back to Colombia, so that his family could see him one last time and say good-bye.

"No, no, no," Don Fernando said to himself. That would cost a fortune, and if he didn't do something right away, those poor souls were going to end up in a common grave somewhere. He was so preoccupied with his thinking that he began to make mistakes as he added and subtracted numbers on the tax documents he was preparing, and had to perform the calculations over and over again before he got them right. Finally he looked up, asked the client he was with to excuse him for a few minutes, and began scrolling through his e-mail in-box for photos of the two kids. He printed them out and slipped them into two transparent folders. He then placed them in front of a box on his desk with a little sign that read COLLECTION FOR BURIAL.

To each and every one of the harried taxpayers who passed through his office that day, he told the tragic story of what he had seen that morning. He told it with such sincerity and poignancy that it seemed like he was telling the story for the first time every time. As they listened to him, men and women alike shuddered at the thought of themselves in the same situation. They shook their heads from side to side, incredulous, as they knocked on wood and thanked God for taking care of their own children. Not a single client left his office that day without leaving a contribution in the makeshift collection box.

"Don Fernando! Don Fernando!" shouted Giovanni, the rowdiest of all his assistants, leaping in front of the people waiting on line. "You gotta get out here! Hurry up, the TV people just got here!"

"You're kidding! Did you see what channel they're from?"

"It's the guys from Channel 22."

"Get out there and see if my Cuban girl is with them!"

"Which Cuban? You mean the one with the big tits and all the cleavage?"

"Call her by her name, you rat."

"Well, what is her name? You mean Sonora, right?"

"That's my girl! She's a real sweetheart! She always does such good news reports. Excuse me for just a minute, I have to go out and say hello to her."

Extricating himself with a bit of effort, the man the newspapers would soon be calling the Pope of Jackson Heights hurried out to the street, slightly flustered.

"Run, run, she's somewhere down that way!" Giovanni egged him on, almost delirious.

"Calm down, calm down, can't you see I'm not twenty years old anymore?"

It wasn't until they reached 79th Street that they finally spied the incomparable silhouette of the popular television reporter who, microphone in hand, was busy interviewing the passersby in front of El Abuelo Gozón, a neighborhood dance hall. A substantial crowd of onlookers—more interested in the reporter's voluptuous figure than her questions—had already gathered around her, vying to get their faces on TV, even for just a moment or two. As soon as the cameras were turned off, Don Fernando made his way through the throng and walked up to her:

"Well, if it isn't Miss Sonora Matancera broadcasting live and on location, right here!"

"*Ave María, caballero!*" she called out.

"Hey, gorgeous! How have you been? What's going on?"

"Don Padrón! How are you? What's new around here?"

"Nothing at all . . . Here I am all alone, abandoned, sad . . . missing you like crazy, sweetheart!"

"Well, I say the same to you, my *gordo bello*," she said, alluding to his portly figure.

"*Bello*, yeah, right! I'm ugly and I know it! I don't buy that for a second; you dumped me like an old pair of shoes, all because I'm fat, old, and ugly!"

Leyla Sonora, the star reporter of Channel 22, had a soft spot for the man who spent all his waking hours doing good deeds. She liked the way he gave absolutely everyone the time of day, the way he looked after all those whom everyone else seemed to have overlooked. In addition to all that, though, he also reminded her of her favorite uncle, a man who had lived in New Jersey since the 1950s, and who had taken care of her and her parents after they had gotten out of Cuba during the chaotic Mariel boat lift. They had lived with him for just over a year, and his house was still the place where she sought refuge every now and then when she needed some affection and support.

That was part of the reason she liked to cover Jackson Heights; she always knew that Fernando would seek her out and lavish her with warmth and kindness. Today, though, he seemed a little more anxious than usual.

"So what brings you here today?"

"We're interviewing people about the mules, and the horrible way they die, Don Fernando."

"Well, that's a coincidence; right now we're trying to raise money for the burial of one of them . . ."

"Hmm . . . do you really think people are going to want to part with their money to pay for a drug trafficker's coffin?"

"Well, why don't you interview me, and you'll see? I'll tell you all about it."

"Are you serious, darling?"

"Absolutely, sweetheart."

"All right, then. Let's get this on tape."

Before they started, the flirtatious reporter adjusted her tight-fitting skirt, double-checked her perfectly lined lips, shook out her long hair, and with a radiant smile offered her viewers a brief introduction to Don Fernando Padrón, which she followed up by saying:

"Now he's going to tell us about the campaign he's kicked off to raise money for the mule's burial."

"Good afternoon, Leyla. I'd like to issue an appeal to anyone and everyone who might be able to help us raise money for a Christian burial for Rafael, a young man from Colombia who is our most recent loss here in the community, and whose death all of us are grieving. Any donation, no matter how small, would be a tremendous help."

"But, Don Padrón, these people know the risks they're taking when they do what they do!"

"Well, I'd say that dying is punishment enough, wouldn't you? How can we allow their families, their loved ones, to suffer even more after all the horrible, unspeakable suffering they've already been through? Can you imagine how devastating it must be for your child to die in a foreign country, and to not be able to bring flowers to his grave?"

"Of course you're right. These families shouldn't have

to pay the price for these tragedies. Thank you for joining us."

Close to midnight, at the end of another long workday, after all his customers and employees had gone home, Fernando himself got ready to go home, to his empty apartment. The mere thought made him feel anxious and sad, so before he left, he emptied the donation jar: almost three thousand dollars. Overcome with emotion, he began to clap his hands and his heart skipped a beat. How very right his good mother had been when she said that helping other people put their lives back together is the only way to get your own life in shape, and that on this great earth there is nothing better, no greater victory than doing good by other people.

As he walked down Manuel de Dios Unanue Place—83rd Street between Baxter and Roosevelt, renamed for the old publisher of *El Diario/La Prensa*, a Basque journalist and friend who had been murdered—a pleasant breeze blew softly in the air. He suddenly felt so lighthearted and jubilant that he actually began to sing an old Colombian *pasillo* called "Espumas," by Jorge Villamil:

"*. . . Espumas que se van / bellas rosas viajeras . . .*" He knew that at that hour there was nobody in Little Colombia who would hear him sing.

The blaring sounds of *Buenos Días, Nueva York* awakened him from the tiny television set that, before going to sleep, he had programmed for six A.M. on the dot. He sat up, and perched at the edge of his bed, he waited. First came the crime news, tons of it, a litany of yellow journalism: suicides, assaults, rapes, and all sorts of grisly crimes. It was a violent breakfast that Leyla served up with tremendous success to a TV audience of hundreds of thousands of Latin Americans.

"Up next, following our commercial break, we'll be back with the latest news from the world of the mules," said the redhead, tilting her head to the right and winking ever so slightly with her right eye. Fernando Padrón settled in and waited for the report that would help him raise the funds he needed to send Rafael's remains back to Colombia.

After the commercials, Leyla Sonora returned and launched into her story:

"And now, here's our latest update: from the Jamaica Hospital morgue, we have Dr. Víctor Murtúa, who spoke with us in this exclusive interview."

"Tell us, Doctor, what was the cause of Juliana Restrepo's death?"

"Cardiac arrest due to a hemorrhage caused by a deep incision in the jugular vein."

"Could you specify what type of object was used to make the incision?"

"Possibly a broken bottle; particles of glass were found in the wound."

"Would you say that Miss Restrepo was a mule, Doctor?"

"I can't comment on police matters. I have to ask you, very specifically, to limit your questions to my field, and not to ask me to speculate in any way."

"Did she show any visible signs of having transported drugs in her body?"

"Not at all."

"Was this young lady a recent arrival from Colombia?"

"Not that I know of; it seems that her assailants confused her with someone else, but the authorities can give you better information about that."

"Have there been any other deaths in the past week related to the drug mafia?"

"Yes, unfortunately. We had one just three days ago."

"Has any contact been made with the family of the deceased?"

"To date, no."

"May we ask the identity of the dead man?"

"Rafael Sarmiento, seventeen years old, from Medellín, Colombia."

"Cause of death?"

"Cocaine overdose due to the rupture of one of the capsules he had been carrying in his stomach."

"Were the other capsules found in his body?"

"Someone else got to them before we did. But that's pretty typical."

"In what condition did you find the body?"

"In a condition that I am sure you can picture if you use your imagination, miss."

To the shock of everyone who had been waiting to see Fernando interviewed on TV, the minutes went by and the face they knew and loved so dearly never appeared on screen. The news report ended, as did the program, and Padrón never turned up. "Did I speak so badly that they couldn't understand me?" he wondered. "Or was it that they just didn't care about what I had to say?"

Oh, well. He would figure out how to get the money he

needed to keep the promise he'd made to the victims' families. In a little while he'd go over to his office to ponder that a little more. Thinking about those things, he turned off the TV set, and wrapping himself up in his sheets and blankets like a baby, he went back to sleep for a little while.

5

The 7 Train: Roosevelt Avenue

As he lifted his head, he was awed by the stunning winter landscape that unfolded before his eyes: Park Avenue covered in snow. Despite this promising first impression, he didn't get much farther than a block before deciding it was pointless to walk the city in those frigid temperatures if he didn't know where he was going. To avoid freezing to death, he decided to go back to where he had started: Grand Central. Sitting on a bench in the enormous train station, he concluded that the best thing to do was seek refuge on one of the trains.

•   •   •

Perhaps it was a premonition that led him to settle in and spend his first night in New York in a toasty car on the 7 train. His eyes and mouth opened wide as he watched the train make its entrance to Queensboro Plaza. He tried to sleep in between the few stops the train made—he had been lucky in that sense, for he had somehow gotten himself on an express train, the kind that made very few stops late at night and on the weekends. His fear of getting mugged, though, kept him from getting a good night's sleep.

Dawn caught him by surprise, up above on the elevated train tracks. He watched as people came on the train with paper cups filled with something that instantly brought him back home: it was the smell of freshly brewed coffee, and it was strong and inviting enough to convince him to get off the train. He quickly found his way out of the station and over to an eclectic little corner kiosk that sold newspapers, coffee, and a strange kind of bread with a little hole in the middle. As time went by he would develop a taste for bagels, preferably toasted, with plenty of cream cheese.

The coffee reminded him of the dark black brew of Medellín; he closed his eyes as he savored the hot drink, and he felt himself transported back to his good mother's kitchen, where he had learned to walk and eat, to read and write, and more than anything else, to be a good man, all thanks to the love of Doña Lucrecia Mendoza, his good mother whose example guided him always, and whom he missed terribly, every moment of the day.

After regaining his strength with the small banquet he'd ordered, Fernando concentrated on the swarms of people who rushed in and out as if they were off to conquer the world or fight a great battle. They were all bundled up in thick sweaters, scarves, hats, overcoats, and gloves. After pondering things for a while, still scared he would end up frozen solid, he decided the moment had come to venture outdoors again. He prayed for the snow to stop. And it did.

Fernando took the 7 train to Times Square and walked to lower Manhattan, all the way to Spring Street. It wasn't until several months later that he actually learned the meaning of the word "spring." When he did he smiled, recalling his first contact with the city he'd dreamed about ever since he was a child. In the future he would occasionally return to Spring Street, and it always brought him back to that winter morning when his new life began.

It had stopped snowing, but the cold had intensified, penetrating deep into his bones. He rubbed his hands together and walked clumsily across the smooth carpet of snow that, at certain points, had frozen into a cold, slippery sheet of ice. He painfully experienced a couple of serious tumbles, the impact of which reverberated all the way up through his cranium like a thunderous blow.

"Relax, man, relax, it's just the beginning," he repeated to himself over and over again with difficulty, since his teeth had begun to chatter uncontrollably. Intuition led him toward a sign that said LITTLE ITALY, where the camaraderie he observed among the people making their way up and down the sidewalk seemed familiar in some way. As he watched the passersby greet each other on their way to the subway, or while waiting for a bus, or as they entered the bakeries along the street, he felt that he was in a friendly, welcoming neighborhood.

That was when he noticed signs in the windows of some of the restaurants, offering jobs for waiters, busboys, and dishwashers. Though they were all closed because it was still very early in the morning, Fernando promised himself that if he couldn't figure out how to get to the blessed island where he was certain his compatriots were enjoying a hot, delicious breakfast in the warm home of Castaño's brother, he would come back here and try to get a job at one of these restaurants. There was no point wallowing in pity, he told himself, shaking his head and banishing the gloomy thoughts that crept into his mind now and then. Instead he decided to continue exploring Little Italy.

Suddenly a giant finger materialized in front of his nose, and someone began speaking to him in elemental Spanish sprinkled with a foreign language that sounded vaguely similar to his own native tongue:

"Forty a week!" bellowed the voice, in between blasts of smoke that streamed out from a thick Havana cigar being puffed by a corpulent Italian man in a gray overcoat, black scarf, and felt hat.

"Excuse me?" asked Fernando, slightly taken aback. Surely the man hadn't been talking to him.

"Forty dollars to work six days a week," said the angel that God had placed in his path. The Italian man went on to make Fernando an offer that, right then, sounded absolutely marvelous. "Ten hours a day with lunch and dinner included. What do you say, *ragazzo*? *Ti piace?*"

Forty dollars seemed like a fortune to Fernando, and he was tempted to shout out "Yes!" without even asking what the job entailed, but he hesitated: he still didn't have a place to live. The man asked him what he was so worried about, and when Fernando explained his predicament, the corpulent Italian smiled and in a paternal tone of voice said, "Don't worry, that's *facile* to fix. The other boys at the restaurant pay *sette* dollars a week for the shared room. If you like, I send you over with a *ragazzo* to help you with your *bagaglio, fatto una doccia calda per iniziare il lavoro.* Your *horario* is from *due* to *dodici* in the night. That is your schedule."

Dumbfounded, Fernando received a couple of slaps on the shoulder when he asked what the work consisted of.

"*Facilíssimo, bambino*, washing the dishes! You can't start out as manager in this country, eh! *Benvenuto a Colombo's, ciccio! Benvenuto a la piccola Italia!*"

In no time at all Camilo, a lively, talkative Mexican, arrived to take Fernando to the subway, where they took the 6 train to the 7 train. This brought them to the building that Fernando would soon call home. For the entire trip, Camilo droned on and on, in an endless monologue about his childhood, his job, and the legendary owner of the restaurant where Fernando would work. They had just stepped off the second train and were walking down the station stairs when the street-smart Mexican suddenly turned to Fernando. "You know who he is, don't you? The man who hired you?" Camilo asked, walking quickly down the street.

"No, I have no idea. I don't know anyone, man. I just got here."

"Well, let me tell you, there's plenty of people who would have killed to be in your shoes today, man . . . I mean you got hired by the big cheese, Pietro Colombo, in person. Damn!"

"If he's the owner of that restaurant, then I guess he must be a millionaire, huh?"

"Not just that restaurant, brother. That old bastard owns half of New York, don't you get it? Don't you get who he is? He's Pietro Colombo, man!"

"Yeah, you said that already. But who is he?"

"He's only the biggest fucking mafioso in town, brother."

Mafioso? Was it true? Was he, Fernando Jeremías Padrón Mendoza, after barely twenty-four hours in New York City, going to work for a mafioso? Had he traveled so far from home, fleeing the memory of Benjamín that had tortured him day and night, only to fall into the same trap as his friend? He couldn't believe that life had dealt him such a cruel blow.

He stopped in his tracks, suddenly feeling as if he were trapped under a coffin. Camilo shook him and shook him, until he finally managed to push Fernando toward a brown brick building. When they reached the apartment, the door creaked open to reveal yet another surprise. Again, Fernando stood still, unable to move, dumbfounded as he contemplated the space that would be his bedroom: a rectangle with eight bunk beds set up in two rows, tightly packed together and neat as a pin. The beds were all covered with homespun bedspreads, and freshly washed clothes from the night before were hanging from a clothesline suspended above the heater, like a bizarre decorating scheme.

The walls were covered with pictures—mostly of voluptuous women in the nude—cut out from posters, magazines, and books. There were snapshots everywhere, of family members, fathers, grandmothers, girlfriends, babies, dogs, cats, and horses; cards from friends in Vietnam; pennants from favorite soccer teams; images of Jesus, María Félix, Rock Hudson, and Gina Lollobrigida; horseshoes, aloe vera and ruda leaves; amulets for protection against envy and the evil eye; inspirational thoughts like "The best revenge is success," or "If you think you've lost, you have"; and numerous images of the Virgin of Guadalupe, Saint Jude Thaddeus, and Saint Martin of Porres.

Fernando took a deep breath before saying anything. Then:

"Am I the first Colombian to come here?"

"What are you, kidding? Listen, *gordito*, here there's no firsts or lasts," Camilo explained, helping him fit his things under the only available bed, which had a mattress but no sheets. "Here we've got guys of every color and from every place in the world."

"So you mean, there's people from my country, too?"

"Of course! Just what I said: there's guys from everywhere, man, we've even got a couple of dudes that you look at them and you'd think they're from a couple of towns away from yours, and then you try and talk to them in Spanish and guess what? These guys are from the end of the earth, way out there in Pakistan, man! Or Bangladesh, imagine that."

"And all of them work down there in Little Italy?"

"Here, there, all over the place. But forget about Little Italy for now, brother, because you're going to work with me right here in Queens Terrace, *gordito*."

"Where's that?"

"Roosevelt and 69th, right here, just around the corner from the building. What do you think, we live here for the scenery?"

"Does Mr. Colombo own this building, too?"

"He owns the air you breathe, man! That's why he's always looking for new guys. You know how many tables there are in our restaurant?"

"I don't know . . . eighty . . . ?"

"Try seven hundred. You're going to dream about dirty dishes by the time you go to bed at night, man!"

"Holy shit!"

"Welcome to the international brigade of the dishwashers!"

Following an ancient custom of unknown origin observed religiously by all dishwashers, the new recruit was always left alone on his first day so that he might break as many plates as possible under the watchful eyes of the veterans, who invariably doubled over laughing at the sight. It was all but impossible not to drop the dishes because, savvy and crafty as they were, the experienced dishwashers always stationed the new guy at the old, rickety machines that belched out more fumes than a locomotive. The plates that came out were so unbelievably hot that there was no way not to get burned as you pulled them out.

Amid the incessant barks of "Faster, faster!" from his supervisor, countless plates went crashing down to the floor those first few days on the job. With his scalded hands, the beginner would then have to grab the broom to sweep up every last shard from the floor, which was littered with bits of garlic, onion skin, shrimp peels, chicken guts, pasta, butter, oil, and tomato sauce. The combination of boiling water and industrial detergent ate away at the skin on the palms of Fernando's hands, and they soon grew as tough as leather. He was shocked by the supersonic speed at which dirty plates were delivered to him; it was as if they grew and multiplied all on their own. The busboys brought the dirty dishes in on huge trays, and immediately took the clean ones out on their speedy little trolleys so that they could set the tables as fast as possible to keep up with the endless stream of customers.

From the very first hesitant step he took on the greasy, slippery kitchen floor, Fernando had the feeling that here, in this tiny, hot little jungle, he might be safe from the slings and arrows of the outside world. Danger, however, seemed to beckon everywhere he looked. The majority of the ostensibly Italian chefs were in fact Mexicans, and their assistants were either from El Salvador, Cuba, Honduras, or Ecuador, but working together did little to forge friendships between them. Whenever they got into arguments and brawls, Fernando had to quickly run for cover because fights were veritable battles between pirates who carried knives so sharp that they could lop off fingers— and they did, on occasion—as easily as they sliced eggplants.

In addition to the culinary utensils that moonlighted as lethal weapons, the kitchen presented other hazards, too:

God forbid a pot of steaming soup, or water for boiling lobsters, or potato fryers filled with scalding oil should topple over on you.

"Why'd you come north, man?" asked Camilo, submerged up to his elbows in murky, soapy water.

"For a better life, what else? To save up money, just like you and everyone else here."

"That's not what I'm talking about, man."

"Well, what then?"

"What are you running away from, buddy?"

"Running away? Me? Nothing."

"Nothing bad happened to you in Colombia?"

"No, nothing. Nothing happened to me. What makes you think that, man?"

"Don't try and fool me, *gordito*. All of us who come up north are running from something. Come on."

"Well, I don't know who 'all of us' is, but I'm not one of them."

"Come on, don't get shy on me now, damn it, I thought you were so cool, so *padre*!"

"*Padre?* That's what I'm like, you think? A father?"

"Don't be such a drag, man, tell me the real story. What happened? Some chick dumped you?"

"No, no, nothing like that."

"I got it, I got it: you came here 'cause you want to get as much action as you can, right?"

"No, man, no!"

"Well, what, then, did you get fired from your job?"

"No! I came because I wanted to!"

"Come on! For real? You didn't come to get out of the military service, did you?"

"No way, man. In fact, when I came here I was all ready to go to war."

"All right, all right, I got it—you got diagnosed with cancer and you've only got two months left to live."

"Yeah, right. You think I'd be washing dishes if that happened to me?"

"Well then, what did you come here for? I think someone died on you, someone you really loved."

"No. Nobody."

"Well, the look on your face says something else."

"Do me a favor and shut up for a little while, Camilo, will you?"

"All right, man, all right, I'll shut up. But on one condition."

"What's that?"

"That you tell me the story of the dead guy who sent you running to New York."

Closing time was the most exhausting part of the workday at the Terrace. They had to contend with mountains and mountains of greasy pots and pans and then haul monstrous quantities of garbage over their shoulders out onto the street. But, like everything, it had its bright side, too, for it was also the hour when the waiters and busboys—who by then had showered, changed, and dabbed themselves with cologne—yelled themselves hoarse arguing over their respective portions of the tips. Others fought over who would take home the most succulent cuts of leftover grilled meat, ham hocks, and turkey breasts. They shared these spoils with families, friends, coworkers, and neighbors, who then saved a fortune in grocery shopping.

Maybe their bosses were sinister, bloodthirsty Mafia kingpins, but one thing was for sure: any employee who performed an honest, hard day's work was well remunerated for his efforts. They were actually required to take home any and all leftovers from the expensive meals they served; throwing food into the garbage was grounds for immediate dismissal. Fernando would never forget what Pietro Colombo had said to him that first day on the street in Little Italy: "Nobody has ever starved to death working in the kitchen at one of my restaurants, *bambino*." This was what convinced Fernando that he couldn't have ended up in a better place:

They had just finished placing hundreds of clean glasses on the shelves in perfectly straight rows, when the mischievous Camilo started in again with all his nosy questions, forcing Fernando to revisit the past.

"What happened, *gordito*, come on . . . Weren't you going to tell me the story about the dead guy?"

"I never said anything about any dead guy."

"What do you mean? You just told me about it before."

"Damn you're pushy. I didn't say anything like that."

"Well, you didn't have to, man. You went pale as a ghost when I asked you."

"You're real sharp, aren't you . . . ?"

"I know how to read people, brother. What can I say?"

"Why do you care so much? Huh?"

"Well, if we're gonna be buddies, we can't have any secrets, *gordito*. Secrets are no good."

"But I just met you! I can't tell the story of my life to a total stranger!"

"Listen, if we don't tell each other the truth, we're never gonna be able to help each other out, know what I mean?"

"What truth? What the hell do you want me to tell you?"

"Who was the guy who died? Your old man?"

"No."

"Your mom?"

"No, thank God."

"So who? Your girlfriend."

"No, man. No."

"All right, I give up, who's the deceased party?"

"A friend."

"A friend! Damn! You left your country all on account of a friend dying?"

"I don't think you understand; he wasn't just any friend."

"Well, yeah, sure, but I still don't get it."

"What happened, to be honest—my friend didn't die, exactly."

"All right, now I really don't understand you, brother."

"He didn't die, Camilo, he was killed."

Very often, it is precisely when everything is going so swell that you have to wonder if it isn't a little too good to be true. After all, as the old saying goes, if you think something's too good to be true, it probably is. That was more or less what happened when Benjamín started wearing fancy clothes, gold chains, and silver rings, even a Nivada watch. Most surprising of all, however, was the gleaming silver Vespa motorcycle that he started riding around town. It was the type of bike that a rich landowner's son would buy to show off how rich he was to all the girls.

"Where did you get the money to buy all that shit?" Fernando asked him, over and over again. But Benja never said a word: he just invited Fernando along with him, changed the topic of conversation, told him stories.

"It's no big deal, *gordito*, no reason to get all worked up, they're just some gifts from an uncle I've got who sends me money from the United States. Boy, you sure jump to conclusions . . ."

"Don't give me that bullshit. . . . Sure, an uncle in the United States who spoils you rotten?" Fernando snapped back. "What do you think I am, an idiot? You're either dealing or turning tricks, or who knows, maybe both."

"Oh, thank you for thinking so highly of me! Do you actually think I'd do that?"

"Well, I can't think of any other explanation. You were always poor, just like me. Where else did it come from, then?"

"Wouldn't that be awesome, if someone paid me to sleep with some lady? Man, I bet you'd do it with me if you had a deal like that!"

"Quit joking and tell me what you're up to, for real."

"Why do you want to know so bad?"

"Because a while ago, you and I swore we would be friends till we died. Or have you forgotten that already?"

"I haven't forgotten, brother, but man, you're more like my mother than my friend. You're worse, even!"

"Why would I try to be your mother, man? And why don't you just tell me already?"

"The way you keep tabs on me, man, it's like I can't live my life!"

"Live your life, man, sure, but it seems like you're just trying to fuck it up."

"Oh, don't be such a downer!"

"Man, you try and help someone and all they do is give you shit for it."

"Come on, you know that I've never felt better than I do now. Why can't you just be happy for me, *gordito*, instead of questioning me all the time?"

"If I'm questioning you, it's because I get the feeling you're up to something that's no good. Tell me the truth, Benjamín. If you can't tell me, who can you tell?"

"Do you really think I'm turning tricks? Or are you just jealous because all the chicks are after me instead of you?"

"Drop it already with all that shit, will you? Now, are you gonna tell me where you're getting all that money or what?"

"No, man, I mean, if I tell you, you're just going to start giving me shit, and then you're gonna go off and tell my old man."

"Oh, so now you're calling me a rat? Now, after all the trouble I got you out of, bastard?"

"All right . . . all right, brother. I'm gonna tell you, but you have to swear you're not going to tell anyone about it. Okay?"

"I swear."

"You have to swear on someone."

"I swear on my mother, on yours, and the Virgin of Monserrate."

"Okay, okay, that's plenty."

"So talk, then."

"It's nothing, man, you said it yourself, I've just started doing a little business around school. That's all."

"Oh, yeah? Selling what?"

"Come on! Don't play dumb with me!"

"Give it to me straight, if you're such a macho man. Come on: what are you selling?"

"All right, so I sell a little weed. Duh! I'm not gonna go around selling sugar water!"

"What did I say? I knew it."

"So why did you have to go and ask me if you already knew?"

"You're not selling your ass, too, are you?"

"Oh, give me a break, will you? Don't insult me, *marica*!"

"It's just that you've got too much money, man. You're gonna tell me that you bought that motorcycle selling pot? You know what? I don't believe you."

"Well, let me repeat what I just said: if you don't believe me, then you're better off not asking in the first place."

"I think you're selling coke, too."

"Ah, it's all the same. I sell what the customers want to buy, brother, that's all."

"What do you mean, 'that's all,' asshole? Your classmates fry their brains while you get rich off of them. That's real nice, huh?"

"Look, if they don't buy it from me, they'll just buy it from the competition, so in the end, it's all the same."

"Oh sure, right. Of course. In the end, who cares? Who cares?"

"When will the day come when you quit telling me off?"

"When you stop talking so much shit that nobody believes, not even you, Benjamín."

Benjamín tried, but he just couldn't figure out how to get his grumpy friend to abandon his sermons and reproaches, and lighten up a little. Finally, he decided to give Fernando a surprise for his birthday: a puppy, a little baby German shepherd, the kind that he had always dreamed about. He was going to the local dog breeder when he found himself strolling past the El Brillante jewelry and pawnshop.

He went crazy the minute he laid eyes on it: a tremendous, 18-karat gold cross that was actually a knife with a curved blade and a razor-sharp, pointed tip. It looked like a military decoration, but one that was tailor-made for a drug dealer or some murder kingpin. It hung from a thick gold chain, smack in the middle of the shop window. In spite of his—and anyone's—better judgment, it was a magnet, a talisman that would have caught the eye of anyone who walked past that shop window. It was the wildest thing in the world. He didn't think twice: his hand went straight to the front pocket of his jeans, and he patted his wad of bills. He then walked straight into the store and, with the air of a gentleman, bought the piece. As cool as a cucumber, he also ordered a luxurious case to go with it, under the suspicious gaze of the baffled proprietor.

At seven o'clock on the eve of his seventeenth birthday, Fernando slipped a coin into the jukebox and the incomparable voice of Celia Cruz filled the bar; it was a happy song that usually managed to perk up his spirits:

"*Se oye el rumor de un pregonar . . .*"

He walked back to the low table where his usual glass of Cola y Pola, a light beer, was waiting for him. He was trying hard to think of other things, but he couldn't help feeling anxious and troubled. His best friend's confession had left him with insomnia for two interminable nights. The music played on.

After a little while, Benjamín made his triumphant entrance into the Taberna Ansiedad. Clowning around with the gift-wrapped package, he perched it just so upon his perfectly slicked-back hair, did a little salsa dance, and as he made a graceful spin around the floor, the back of his blue linen jacket fluttered up in the air.

"Happy birthday, *gordito picarón*!" the recent arrival said, grabbing his friend and locking him in a bear hug, just like soccer players did after scoring a goal.

"Thanks, man, but I'm not there yet. What's that thing on your head? You look like one of those ladies selling vegetables, you nut!"

"*También traigo albahaca pa' la gente flaca,*" Benjamín sang along, rubbing his belly.

"Very funny. Why don't you tell me what you've got there and stop playing dumb."

"It's just a little something, just a little trinket, nothing, really."

"Why do you go around inventing shit? Come on. You don't have to give me anything."

"Listen, I will give you the gifts I feel like giving

you, you hear me? Or do you want to start another fight?"

"All right, man. Thanks. What is it?"

"Open it and you'll see!"

Slowly, gingerly, Fernando removed the ostentatious wrapping, careful not to rip any of the paper. When he realized what was inside he went pale. Quickly, nervously, he wrapped it back up in a hurry, as if he had been given a poisonous spider instead of the valuable item Benjamín had procured.

"You should see the look on your face, man! What's the matter, don't you like it?"

"Now I know you've gone crazy."

"Crazy? What's wrong with it?"

"This shit must have cost a fortune!"

"Nah."

"But, but—what the hell is going on in your head, man? Why do you do these things, huh?"

"I want you to have a memento to remember me by, you know?"

"To remember you . . . Where are you going? A memento for what?"

"I don't know . . . for when we go our separate ways and we don't see each other anymore."

"But you and I live half a block away from each other! We're always going to see each other, don't be ridiculous!"

"That's what you say now, but who knows what's gonna happen tomorrow?"

"How about instead of getting all tragic on me, you return that crazy shit? Right now, Benjamín, right now!"

While Fernando waited for him at the bar, a chagrined Benjamín arrived at the door to El Brillante, but he didn't go in. He unbuttoned his shirt, took the cross out of his pocket, and hung it around his neck. A bitter smile came over his face as he gazed at his reflection in the shop window: just when he had thought he had behaved most splendidly, Fernando had made him feel dirty and scorned, like a criminal.

He was afraid, afraid that one day the people who loved him would forget all about him. That was why he left his name everywhere he went: "Benjamín was here," he scrawled on bus seats, on tree trunks, on fresh blocks of cement on the sidewalk, in the bathrooms at school. "One day I'm going to disappear and nobody will remember me," he said to himself, as a kind of explanation. Or maybe it was a premonition.

As he walked, he could feel the golden dagger bounce lightly against his chest, and he felt himself sink into a pool of negativity: why bother to worry about other people and give them everything he had, if they were only going to turn around and treat him like a piece of trash? His money was no good, it was ill-gotten, contaminated, and that's why they rejected him. He would have expected that reaction from everyone except his unconditional friend: the other half of the inseparable ones. Who ever thought up that stupid nickname, anyway? Nobody was inseparable, nobody was indispensable.

"From then on, the inseparable ones no longer exist," Benjamín thought as he climbed onto a packed bus.

"So what did you do?" Camilo asked.

"I waited for him for hours."

"And what happened?"

"He never came back. At midnight, there I was and nobody came to wish me a happy birthday."

"Did you look for him?"

"Everywhere. In the morning I went all over town looking for him, but nobody knew where he'd gone."

"And the next day?"

"Nothing."

"When did you see him again?"

"Never."

"Never, what do you mean 'never'?"

"Never. I never saw him alive again."

As he stepped off the bus, Benjamín was positive that he'd seen two men—pretty creepy-looking and a lot older than him—following him. He briefly considered making a scene at the bus stop, causing a commotion, taking advantage of all the other people there. But he knew why those men were after him. He started to panic and broke into a run. The two men started to run, too, until they finally cornered him in a dark alley. They grabbed him by the neck and subdued him with no trouble at all.

They said they had come on behalf of the Jabalí—the wild boar—to collect the money from that week's sales. Benjamín started crying, begging them for mercy, and told them that he had spent all the money on a cross for his mother, who was very sick. Two days later a couple of country peasants found his body, peppered with bullets, facedown beneath the relentless sun, down beneath a cliff. The only place Fernando found solace was in his mother's kitchen. The warm, enveloping silence of that space made him feel so safe, so secure.

6
Victims

The coffin that teetered ever so slightly, resting on the shoulders of several men and women, was surrounded by hundreds of people, most of whom were carrying lit candles, white flowers, or huge signs that expressed the anger and indignation they felt:

"Spineless murderers!"

"Stop killing our kids!"

"No more violence!"

The tight, compact procession was illuminated by the morning sun that filtered down through the branches of the leafy cedar trees.

"We're going to air: three, two, one," announced the cameraman, focusing on one of the gravestones to adjust his lens.

Dressed in a dignified, steel-gray suit, the reporter smoothed out her jacket and brushed away a lock of red hair that covered part of her face. Looking straight into the camera, she launched into her report:

"Good afternoon, everyone. This is Leyla Sonora with a special edition of *Buenos Días Nueva York*. On this sad morning we are transmitting live from Calvary Cemetery in Queens, bringing you the details of Juliana Restrepo's burial. This young Colombian woman was savagely murdered just a few days ago, a brutal act presumed to have been carried out by hit men involved in the drug trafficking trade. From the early dawn hours, hundreds of people of all ages—men, women, and children, entire families, mostly Hispanic, from Jackson Heights—have congregated here to express their grief and repudiation of this crime. This is also their way of staging a peaceful but vehement protest against the wave of criminal activities that have targeted the young people of this neighborhood."

Standing off to the side just a short distance away was Jack Londoño, the veteran NYPD detective overseeing the case. With a bouquet of white flowers in his hands, he began to walk through the crowds as if he were just another well-wisher, but in reality he was trying to find some kind of clue to get his investigation rolling. Despite his considerable height and frame, Jack somehow managed to avoid drawing attention to himself. He kept a low profile at all times.

A native of Puerto Rico, Londoño had arrived in New York with the goal of becoming the best investigator in the metropolitan area. By now, he had a fair number of major victories under his belt, but in recent years fatigue and apathy had taken their toll, and he hadn't solved an important case in some time. He was determined, once and for all, to break this bad spell—a spell that constantly reminded him of his impending retirement.

"Good morning, Detective Londoño," the journalist Hernán Torroja called out, slapping him on the shoulder from behind. "Nice to see you."

"Morning," Jack answered drily. In general he despised reporters, but he had a particular distaste for the manipulative scavengers of yellow journalism like Torroja. The few times he had read *Escrutinio*, the free newspaper Torroja had been running for the past several years, he had written it off as nothing but a sensationalist rag. In his opinion, the man was slime.

"So, what new leads are you working on?" Torroja attacked, trying his best to sound benign.

"None, for the moment. But I am completely certain that when I do come up with something, you'll be the last person I talk to about it."

"Ha, ha. You're in a bad mood today, aren't you, sir?"

"I'd really like it if you would just leave me in peace, Torroja."

"I'm sure you would, but I have to warn you that I have a couple of tiny bits of information from a veeeery good source. Would you be interested?"

"No, thanks."

"I've got proof that that no-good Fernando Padrón is using the mules' dead bodies to send money back to drug lords in Colombia."

"Listen, Torroja, I am trying to be polite with you: I'm not interested in your information. Got it?"

"Sattui, the guy from the funeral parlor, is his accomplice. Between the two of them, they fill the dead bodies up with money, as if they were suitcases. That's the real reason for all that charity, don't you get it?"

"With your permission, Torroja, another time. All right?"

As he marched along with the funeral cortege, Fernando stared straight ahead, not looking up to catch Sonora's eye. Coco Sattui walked alongside him with a heavy heart. Then, suddenly, he grabbed Fernando's arm and whispered that he needed to speak with him urgently. "He's going to try and charge me more money," thought Fernando, trying to think up an excuse to get out of it.

Silently, Londoño followed their every move, wondering if that rather phantasmagoric figure was in fact the same embalmer that Torroja had mentioned, and if it was at all worth keeping an eye on him. Sattui and Fernando stopped at the foot of a tree to have a little chat. Their arms crossed, one put his hand on the other's shoulder, and they talked for a few minutes, alternately agreeing or disagreeing by nodding or shaking their heads.

The priest was issuing a particularly heartfelt prayer for the dead girl when suddenly, the Channel 22 mobile unit revved up and tore out of the cemetery so fast that its tires made a loud, screeching noise against the asphalt. Many of the people in the crowd jerked their heads up and stared at one another, speechless. What on earth had made the news team leave so abruptly?

• • •

The old woman, barefoot and wearing a flowered suit, looked as if she were enjoying a peaceful, restful bit of slumber. Her white hair, held together by a tortoiseshell clip, was gathered in a bun at the nape of her neck. Everything about her exuded serenity, despite the yellow tape that had been used to cordon off the crime scene. A police department illustrator was painstakingly recording it all on paper. In a matter of minutes, a large group of police department officials, along with the hotel security detail, had swooped down on the cold room—number 305, of the Red Roof Inn just off the exit to La Guardia Airport. The paramedics who had arrived armed with oxygen tanks, defibrillators, and other resuscitation equipment were left with nothing to do but fill out the death certificate for this anonymous traveler. The old woman had neither passport nor suitcase.

"Is she dead, Officer? Is she dead?" asked Leyla, extending her arm over the shoulder of a security guard in an attempt to get her microphone close to the police officer.

"Affirmative," he replied, not even removing his sunglasses.

"Is this another homicide?"

"We can't know for sure, but it seems likely."

"Do you have any idea of the victim's approximate age?"

"Not the foggiest, miss."

"What kind of heartless monster could kill a poor, defenseless old lady?"

"That's what we're all asking ourselves, miss."

Just then, two heavyset orderlies entered and placed

the old woman's body on a stretcher, and then covered her with a turquoise-colored sheet. Efficient and swift, they whisked her out of the room and down the hall toward the elevator, amid a flurry of curious onlookers.

"What morgue are you taking her to?" Sonora asked, obstinate as ever. "Where are you taking her?"

"Jamaica Hospital," they replied in unison.

"Shit!" shouted one of the cameramen as he tripped over a tangle of cables and tumbled halfway down the stairs in front of him. The camera, which was now cracked open down the middle, followed its master, until they both landed with a thud in the stairwell below.

Fernando was furious: he had just read the headline of the newspaper that Coco had handed to him. He knew how much Torroja hated him, but he never thought the man could be capable of doing something so despicable. This was the last straw. Ashen-faced and unable to utter a word, he rubbed his eyes. When he opened them again he saw his image plastered on the front page of *Escrutinio*, the star subject of a macabre story: FERNANDO PADRÓN, TRAFFICKER OF THE DEAD: REPLACES GUTS WITH DOLLAR BILLS.

His legs were trembling so violently that he began to slide down the tree trunk he was leaning against. He finally fell to the ground, his head in his hands.

"Calm down, Don Fernando, calm down," said Sattui, trying to console him. "We're going to fix this together, don't you worry."

"Can't you see, that rotten jerk has just buried me alive?"

"Look, you can't let something like this run your life!"

"But still, there'll always be people who'll question me . . . God damn that Torroja!"

"Don Padrón, don't exaggerate, it's just a low-rent rag."

"Oh, sure, it's real easy to keep calm when the other guy's the one in trouble, isn't it?"

"Well, no, actually. Take a look at page three. You're not the only one involved."

"Oh, my God, they mixed you up in this, too? What a lowlife!"

"Well, who else would make a better accomplice than me? I cut up the dead bodies and stuff them with the money you give me."

"Don't even joke about it!"

"You need to just laugh it off, Don Padrón, I'm telling you."

"Well, I don't find it funny; I've never laid a finger on anyone in my life. You know that, don't you?"

"Don't go making a tragedy out of something like this, Don Padrón. This is nothing."

"You think it's nothing to call me a trafficker of dead bodies in the newspaper that everyone in the community reads? What could be worse?"

"Calling you a pedophile in a newspaper that everyone in the country reads. What about that?"

"I don't know what you're talking about."

"I'm talking about me, my friend, I'm talking about me."

"Don't tell me that happened to you?"

"Yes, sir. That's why I had to leave Mexico for good."

"My God, what a nightmare! Who would have accused you of such a thing, some girl?"

"Worse. A boy."

"One of your students?"

"No, the son of a neighbor. I gave him piano lessons twice a week. A kid, thirteen or fourteen years old."

"A baby . . . what the hell happened?"

"Well, they say he started getting depressed, quiet, sad, didn't talk to anyone, so his parents took him to see a psychologist . . ."

"And?"

"Well, after a number of sessions, the kid confessed that he had been abused, you know? They ran the medical tests they were supposed to, and they discovered it was true: that the kid had been abused."

"Sweet Jesus!"

"There was an investigation, and they questioned the boy, but it seems that he was too afraid to admit who had done it to him. The detectives interviewed his cousins, his older friends in the neighborhood, until one of the older kids told the police that he was sure I was the rapist because everyone knew I was a *joto*."

"*Joto?* Is that what they call . . ."

"I think you get the picture, Don Fernando."

"Of course, of course, understood."

"I've always been a little crazy, I dress a little extravagantly . . ."

"A little, yeah, sure, but that doesn't mean anything."

"The boy himself stated that I had never tried to touch him, but it didn't matter: people started treating me like a criminal, they interrogated me, humiliated me. And to top it off, a couple of the agents took some terrible photos of me and then turned around and sold them to the newspapers."

"Then what?"

"Well, one day I woke up and saw my face on all the front pages, and in big letters the headlines said, 'This is the degenerate.'"

"My God, Coco, I had no idea that you'd been through anything like that."

"They ruined my life, Don Padrón, they humiliated me and destroyed everything. That's why I had no other choice. I had to leave everything behind and come here."

"Did they take you to trial?"

"Of course. It was agony."

"Oh, my God! What happened then?"

"I was acquitted; my innocence was proved."

"Sooner or later the truth comes out. Why did you leave, then?"

"Oh, the bad smell lingers, Don Fernando. No matter how hard I tried, I just couldn't live with that memory hanging over my head. Looking back, though, I shouldn't have let the whole thing bother me so much. I should have just laughed it off and not let it ruin my life. That's the best approach to this type of situation."

What was Padrón really after with all those campaigns, raffles, and collection boxes? That was the big question in Londoño's head. What for, and in exchange for what? What kind of nut would go around collecting random dead bodies that nobody gives a damn about? Wasn't it a little too good to be true? A little strange, just a little suspicious?

Sitting in front of his computer monitor with a cup of hot coffee, Londoño launched an information search on philanthropist Fernando Padrón. He was convinced that he would find this guy's dark side. This kind of saint just didn't exist. He had to be hiding something: a police record, pending trials, debts, unacknowledged children, back taxes—there had to be some kind of funny business in there.

The first items he read were dozens of articles about Padrón in a number of different newspapers, all of which spoke of him in the most glowing terms. Next, Londoño sent e-mails to the Colombian consulate and other official entities: the board of elections, the police department, his own special investigative unit, asking for all existing information. But all he turned up were the most positive references, signed by the highest authorities: "He is an exemplary man," was how they responded to every question. "The Colombians can be—and are—very proud of him."

Damn it. The challenge was proving more difficult than he thought. Next, he flipped through Padrón's bank account: all he found there were some modest savings, and when he did a nationwide property-title search under Padrón's name, he still came up with nothing.

Suddenly, the phone rang. Lost in his thoughts, Jack let the machine pick up: "You have reached the office of Detective Jack Londoño of the NYPD. At this moment I can't come to the phone. Please leave a message after the beep. Thank you." A young man with a choked-up voice said, "The lady from the Red Roof is named Elvira Verdesoto."

The inspector lunged for the telephone, but all he heard was the other person hanging up.

"What lowlifes!" Murtúa said, fuming. He slammed his hand against the table and sent scalpels and tweezers flying through the air. His two assistants stood still, unsure of what to do. Never had they seen their boss react like this. What they didn't know was that the instant Murtúa looked down at that sweet face, all he could think of was his aunt Doña Georgina. The elderly aunt had raised him after he had been orphaned in the dirt-poor village of Mamara, in the foothills of the Peruvian Andes.

The forensic pathologist couldn't believe his eyes. What kind of animal was capable of committing such an abominable act of cruelty? He furrowed his brow, well lined with wrinkles. How long would these despicable people continue to kill their fellow man, safe in the knowledge that they would be protected by the poverty of others? Throwing his gloves and his apron down on the table, he stormed out of the laboratory, slamming the door as he headed for his office. His aides remained motionless, shocked and saddened by the kindly face of the angelic old woman who seemed to smile ever so slightly as the mountain of cocaine capsules fell from her open belly.

The doctor fell into his easy chair, sighing as he picked up the telephone and dialed one of the few numbers he knew by heart:

"Modus Vivendi Funeral Home, good afternoon."

"Hello. Is this Sattui?"

"None other, Doctor."

"I'm so glad I found you. I need your help."

"At your service, sir."

"I've just come across a terrible case, very possibly the worst I've ever seen."

"What is it?"

"Please come here—you'd be doing me a huge favor. I promise that I wouldn't bother you if it weren't urgent."

"Don't worry, Víctor, that's what I'm here for."

"Thank you, Coco, and please, hurry."

"I'll get there as fast as I can."

Crouching down in the bushes, Hernán Torroja waited until Doña Leonor reached her minivan before he went over to express his condolences. He went on to explain that he was a good friend of Don Fernando's, and had helped raise money. He was a great admirer of Fernando's work, and always tried to help out in whatever way he could. Touched, Doña Leonor thanked him and said that she never could have given her daughter a proper Christian burial had it not been for the generosity of so many good people, many of whom she didn't know personally.

"It was the least we could do, ma'am. You know, us Latinos are used to helping each other out," he said philosophically, half turning around as if he were about to leave.

"Oh, don't leave, sir," she implored. "Some close friends of mine are coming over to have a coffee at my house. Why don't you join us?"

"It would be an honor, Doña Leonor," Torroja responded, his eyes gleaming.

An infiltrator among strangers, the one-man orchestra of *Escrutinio* climbed up to the third floor of Doña Leonor's building, thinking of Fernando, the man whom he gratuitously considered his archenemy. He imagined the countless trips Fernando had made up and down the stairs to his own fourth-floor apartment in the same building.

"What am I doing here?" he asked himself. "What am I going to get out of this little visit? I can tell already, everyone is just going to sit around talking about what a saint the dead girl was."

His question was answered faster than he anticipated: as Doña Leonor prepared the coffee in the kitchen with some of her lady friends, the men in the living room began to float their theories, in very low voices, about the real reason Juliana had been killed.

"They tried to rape her and she put up a fight," said one of them.

"Come on, what are you, kidding? That was a drugged-out gang, a bunch of scumbags who were pissed off because she didn't have any money on her," said another one.

"All of you are lost in space, man," said a third person. "What happened is that the mafia confused her with a coke dealer who looked exactly like her, some kid who thought she was real clever and tried to pull a fast one on them."

Torroja was starting to get annoyed at himself. This was turning out to be a big waste of his time—time he could have spent a lot better inventing new stories. But then suddenly Don Ramón, the oldest of the group, stood up. A bald man who spoke like a university professor, Don Ramón issued the following ominous statement:

"Listen, my friends, what I am about to tell you must not leave this room. They didn't mix Juliana up with anyone. She got something she's had coming to her since she arrived five years ago with cocaine in her stomach. She didn't hand it over. She kept it, sold it, and pocketed the money."

Nobody moved. Nobody dared to contest the shocking

revelation. Don Ramón's voice lowered to a whisper as he told them the rest of the story.

"They were waiting for her in Miami but she changed planes and entered through Atlanta. She eliminated the drugs without a problem and then sold them on her own, earning around thirty thousand dollars for herself. Then she used that money to bring her mother and two sisters to the States. The rest of it she sent back to her two little boys, who stayed in Colombia with her mother-in-law."

"Why didn't she bring her kids over, too?" Torroja asked. The others had no idea who he was, really, but they didn't bother to question him.

"She was terrified the dealers would take their revenge out on her kids. In fact after she left Colombia her whole family packed up and moved to another city. They all knew what she had done, even Leonor."

"But . . . to kill her just like that, out of nowhere, so many years later . . ."

"The mafia, man, they're like elephants, they never forget," Don Ramón said.

Now, there's a good idea for tomorrow's headline, Torroja said to himself, smiling a tight, private little smile to himself.

As he entered Fernando Travel, Londoño found its proprietor indulging in a succulent lunch of pork shoulder with rice, beans, and fried plantains. As always, he was surrounded by a throng of people in need of assistance. It was a colorful scene that, in and of itself, would have been more than enough to captivate Londoño, but before he could even utter a greeting or introduce himself to Padrón, he was intercepted by two older women gussied up in flamboyant multicolored shirts and beach hats, smiling broadly, a rather incongruous welcome committee that instantly accosted him with the following friendly greeting:

"Nice to meet you! I'm Eva!"

"And I'm Fanny!"

"But the world knows us as . . ."

"*Otoño y Primavera!*"

Jack didn't quite know how to respond to the two ladies whose nicknames represented, respectively, autumn and spring. But he did his best to be as gentlemanly and polite as possible—after all, either of these two ladies could easily be his mother.

"Lovely to meet you, ladies, my name is José," he lied.

"What country are you from, José?" Fanny asked.

"I'm from Venezuela," he replied, lying again.

"Venezuela, Fanny!" exclaimed Eva.

"Well, then . . . 'Caballo Viejo,' " she replied. " 'Caballo Viejo.' I love that song!"

"Excuse me?" asked Londoño, amused. By way of an answer, the two ladies suddenly burst into song:

> *Cuando el amor llega así de esa manera*
> *Uno no se da ni cuenta . . .* *

Everyone in the tiny storefront burst out in a unanimous ovation, and sang along to the popular Venezuelan song, keeping time by clapping their hands. As the harmonious

---

* *When love arrives like that/A person doesn't even realize it.*

matronly duo continued singing, the slightly embarrassed detective looked on with fascination as Fernando covered one ear, and simply went on doing what he was doing, answering the telephone, gesticulating as he glanced down at his watch, and taking rapid-fire notes, undisturbed by the impromptu performance. Londoño wasn't able to hear what he was saying or read his lips, so instead he just watched as Fernando ordered his young employees around like the captain of a ship: first, Daniel grabbed the car keys and raced out of the office; next, Giovanni sat down in front of the computer and his fingers began to fly over the keyboard as he executed a series of searches on the Internet. All with the dulcet tones of Fanny and Eva in the background.

"Mr. Padrón," Londoño ventured. "Excuse me, but I need to ask your help with something."

"I'm sorry, son, right now I can't help you with anything. They just called me about a poor old grandma who turned up dead somewhere, and I'm busy."

"The lady from the Red Roof Inn near La Guardia?" Fernando looked up, surprised.

"That's right, how did you know?"

"Her name is Elvira Verdesoto."

"God almighty! Are you sure? Who are you?"

"That doesn't matter right now. Let's do something."

"We gotta look that name up everywhere, kid."

"How can I help?"

"You know how to use the Internet?"

"Sure."

"Click onto the link that says 'Consulate of Colombia,'" Fernando instructed.

"Right. Okay. They want a password."

"Write my name backwards."

"Easy enough. Now?"

"Click where it says 'Register of Colombian Citizens in the United States' and in the box write the lady's name."

"Let's see, let's see . . . nothing."

"All right now, go to the link that says 'Bogotá White Pages.'"

"Damn, Fernando. You're a real private eye."

"Hey, if you're gonna help, fine, but don't get smart with me. All right?"

"No, no, on the contrary. What I meant to say was, that with all due respect, sir, next to you Hercule Poirot is a fool."

Leyla Sonora was beside herself; she had to cover the story of the old lady, and she didn't know what to do. There was no way she could call Dr. Murtúa after the little trick she had pulled on him the other day. The minute he laid eyes on her he would call the cops. Fernando was out too: he was angry at her and with good reason.

"Oh, who can I go to, who can I go to?" she asked herself, fidgeting as she sat in her mobile TV unit, parked in front of the morgue. Then, suddenly, she saw Coco Sattui quickly turn the corner, almost running.

In a flash Leyla shot out of the van and practically pounced on him, but every single one of her questions was met with the same response:

"Go and talk to Don Fernando first."

Irritated, she climbed back into the TV van and told the driver, "Let's get out of here."

•   •   •

Murtúa went out to greet his visitor and quickly escorted him to the room where the little old lady was, once again surrounded by criminal experts who were meticulously examining her, fascinated by what they saw.

As soon as he took in the bloodcurdling scene, Sattui burst into silent tears, probably thinking back to someone from somewhere in his old life, God only knew who. Gently stroking the old lady's white hair, Sattui promised Dr. Murtúa that he would make sure her body got back to Colombia safe and sound, looking exactly like the angel she must have been when she was alive.

"He's gonna tell me to go to hell," Leyla thought as they drove toward Fernando Travel, imagining the sour face that she was going to have to contend with if Fernando Padrón even agreed to speak to her.

"Ave María, look who we have here!" Fernando cried out as he saw Leyla Sonora approach him with a contrite look on her face.

"Do you know this young lady here?" Fernando asked Londoño, who smiled as he looked at her, and replied, "There isn't a single person in this town who doesn't know that face."

"Good afternoon, everyone," Leyla called out gaily. Once recognized, she was greeted with a very Cuban serenade, courtesy of Otoño and Primavera.

Qué manera de quererte, qué manera![*]

---

[*]*Oh, how I love you, oh how!*

"My goodness! What beautiful voices, ladies!" said the well-known television reporter. "Thank you so much!"

"Let me guess," said the owner of Fernando Travel. "You want to interview me again, right?"

"Oh, *gordito*, don't be like that with me, don't be so mean, I can barely look you in the face as it is. I'm so sad about what happened!"

"Sad, come on! Don't try to put one over on me, lady, you aren't one bit sad and you know it."

"I know you're upset with me, honey, but I swear I will do anything to make it up to you."

"You shouldn't go around promising things you can't deliver."

"Whatever you say, I swear!"

"Well, I don't know. You know what they say about the boy who cried wolf . . ."

"Oh, won't you give me another chance, *gordito*, pretty please?"

"Another chance for what?"

"Oh, come on, you know I need your help."

"Well, I just happen to need you, too."

"I'm talking about the old lady they found," said Leyla.

"Me, too."

"I don't get it."

"Oh, so now you're playing dumb."

"But how can I help you if you're the one who knows everything around here?"

"I've only just started investigating, Leyla, but an idea just occurred to me."

"Whatever you say."

"My good friends here are the well-known group Otoño

y Primavera. I'm sure you've heard of them," said Fernando.

"Of course I have! They're fabulous! Everyone loves them!"

"Fine, now listen: what would you say if I told you they are going to give a concert to raise money for the burial of that little old lady?"

"I'd say it's a great idea!"

"We'll charge five bucks per person and we'll do it at Natives on Northern Boulevard. We're going to have to pack the house, though, and there's no way we can do that without your help."

"Well, I'll make sure to promote it on my show. I promise you."

"Great."

"You have my word. Now, won't you help me out with your friend Murtúa? I have to get into that morgue, no ifs, ands, or buts. I have to get more information on that case."

"I'm not falling for that one twice, honey. First I am going to watch your show tomorrow. Then I will help you with whatever you want."

Giovanni went down to the basement canteen, walked over to the counter, and ordered two Colombianas and an Inca Kola, signing for them in a notebook kept for those trusted customers who were allowed to run a tab. As always, he flirted a little with the girl behind the counter. Today, however, as he turned around to go back up to the office, he felt a hand press down on his shoulder.

"You're Padrón's assistant, aren't you?"

"My name is Giovanni, Mr. Torroja."

"Oh, wow, so you know who I am."

"Around here, everyone knows who you are, man."

"You don't say. And is that good or bad?"

"For humanity, good. For you, terrible."

"Real funny, kid, but I'm not here for fun, okay? Now run along and tell your big boss that the newspaper *Escrutinio* is still waiting for the prestigious Fernando Travel to take out an ad in our pages as soon as possible. If not . . ."

"If not, what?"

"If not we're going to have to keep reporting the very worst news about him to our readers."

"Are you serious? Is that what you want me to tell him?"

"I have never been more serious in my life."

"Well, I'm very sorry, Mr. Torroja, but there's no way you're going to get me to give Don Fernando that kind of message. If you want to blackmail him, you're going to have to do it yourself."

As a strategy it had never worked, but whenever people died carrying drugs, the police held on to the bodies until further notice. The idea was to keep the dead person as a kind of hostage so that the relatives—and presumed accomplices—would come forward to the authorities. If they did, they would be immediately arrested, on charges of drug trafficking.

"I can't believe you would be this inhuman!" Murtúa bemoaned. "At least let us prepare the body so that we can send it home after we locate the family members!"

The police were adamant: as long as the investigation was open, that body wouldn't move an inch until someone came in person to claim it. Sattui, broken up by what had happened to the old lady, offered to come to the morgue with his mortician's instruments so that he could embalm her without having to remove her from the premises. Suddenly a forensic assistant interrupted their conversation:

"Doctor, there's a call for you."

"Hello? Hello?" barked Murtúa, testy as always.

"I killed her," said the voice at the other end, collapsing in sobs. "It was me. I killed her."

"What . . . ? Who is this?"

"I made her swallow all those drugs, I sent her to the slaughterhouse, oh, God, you are never going to forgive me for this, I'm a murderer!"

"Please, try and calm down, sir, whoever you are."

"She was afraid, but I forced her, I told her she had to make a sacrifice for her little grandson . . ."

"You're calling me from Colombia, aren't you?"

"She loved her grandson more than anything in the whole world, and I knew she would do anything for him."

"Didn't you know that you were setting her up for the most hellish death imaginable?"

"I didn't mean to hurt her, but we're dying of hunger here, and they told me nothing would happen to her, that since she was a little old lady nobody would suspect her of anything, they told me it would be real simple and that everything would come out okay . . ."

"So you wanted to make a bunch of money trafficking drugs, is that it? Why didn't you bring them over here yourself in your own rotten belly, you disgusting coward?"

"Oh, God, where is she? We have to bury her here, in

her village, she can't just end up out there, anywhere. Have you seen her?"

"Of course I've seen her, you miserable pig!"

"Tell me, tell me, how is she?"

"How do you think she is? Lying out on a slab with her guts hanging out, like a frog!"

"Oh, my God, my God! Please don't say that! Don't say that! Forgive me, forgive me, *Mamá*!" The ensuing crash told Murtúa that his interlocutor had ended the painful conversation.

Without even thinking about it, Murtúa dialed the number of Fernando Travel, tapping his pen against the desk as he waited for someone to pick up. As soon as he heard Fernando's voice at the other end, he implored,

"Please, Fernando, come down here as quickly as possible, I need to talk to you." Then he hung up, leaving Fernando speechless.

Fernando instantly jumped up from his chair and looked at the clients lined up to see him:

"Listen," he said, "I'm sorry but I have to leave now because of an emergency." The men and women looking at him knew: the services of the guardian angel of Jackson Heights covered a very broad territory.

In silence they helped him clean up and get on his way.

7
Big Brother
_____

Years later the little boy holding on to his mother's hand would write:

"It was a sunny day, and it was still very cold outside when Mommy told me to wash up good and put on my best clothes. 'Why?' I asked her. She explained that I was going to meet a man that afternoon who was going to be like my big brother. 'Who is he?' I asked her, but she wasn't sure herself. All she knew was that he had been recommended by the people at school, that we would be spending a few hours together, and that she would pick me up afterward to take me home. 'What if I don't like him?' I asked. 'You'll like him,' she said, adding: 'And anyway, he's going to take you out for lunch.' 'Whatever I want?' I asked. Back in those days, I was always hungry; at home the meals were few and the portions small . . .

"When I arrived at the little storefront where a large group of people waited on a line to talk to the man who I would later call my 'big brother,' I went numb. How long was I going to have to wait to get a good meal?"

Even though it was well past one in the afternoon on Saturday, Fernando Travel was still packed with people waiting their turn. The little boy, somewhat bewildered by the sight, bid good-bye to his mother, a woman around thirty-five, who then closed the door and crossed the street. Once inside, the little boy surveyed the line of people and decided it would take an eternity to finally meet the man he was there to see. He rummaged through his backpack and pulled out *The Sword in the Stone*, part one of the tetralogy entitled *The Once and Future King*. Danielito opened the book and time passed faster than he thought it would.

Once he was finally sitting down in front of Fernando's desk, with perfect posture and a backpack big enough to carry a bookshelf full of books, Danielito broke into a smile so big that it lit up his entire face. You could feel the energy and enthusiasm that made his heart race so fast: he seemed to have a very pressing need to communicate something, but unlike most of the people who waited around for Fernando, this little boy seemed filled with joy and happy things he simply wanted to share with someone. Smiling, Fernando looked down at him with a quizzical look on his face, which the child read right away:

"Hi. Are you Don Fernando?"

"At your service."
"I'm your little brother."
"What's that?"
"You're my big brother!"

Fernando's initial hesitation suddenly evaporated, replaced by a smile of pure delight as he remembered how, weeks earlier, at a reception in honor of the local chapter of Big Brothers/Big Sisters, he had offered to be a big brother to a Hispanic child. Being a big brother or sister to a young kid was part of that very American tradition of volunteering, an admirable undertaking that Latin Americans were not very familiar with. At the reception, Fernando had decided to do something to help change the perception that Latin Americans were people who didn't participate in community activities.

And anyway, he really did think it was a worthwhile effort: as a big brother, he could have a real impact on the life of a child and perhaps prevent him from getting mixed up in a life of crime as an adolescent. According to what they said at the reception, one out of every three Hispanic kids left school at the elementary level. He knew they were ripe pickings for those who specialized in getting their hands on the young for unsavory pursuits. No matter how busy he was, Fernando vowed to do whatever he could to help save at least one of those kids.

There was something else, too: despite all the work that filled his days and nights, Fernando had never managed to fill the hole left behind by the absence of his little niece and nephews. After their falling-out, his sister Patricia forbade the children from getting in touch with their uncle. He missed them terribly; every single day things happened that he yearned to share with them. After all, he had known them since the day they were born, and had watched them grow up.

And so, after giving it some serious thought, he said yes to the Queens area program coordinator who called him up to see if he would be willing to be a big brother. Mr. Triana was a native of Madrid and had been with the organization for over twelve years. He knew all about Fernando's work with the Latin community in Jackson Heights. Thanks to this, he agreed to break the protocol which dictated that "brothers" should go on outings. The little boy's mother would leave her son at Fernando Travel on Saturday afternoons because she had a job nearby. This worked out perfectly for Fernando because it allowed him to get ahead with his own work. Everything was settled, then: Danielito would show up at Fernando Travel at around one in the afternoon.

Fernando's little brother arrived like a gift from the heavens above; as he looked at Danielito, Fernando thought of his mother, Doña Lucrecia, and felt that she, too, would have been content with his decision.

"Tell me, what's your name?"

"Daniel, Don Fernando, but my mother calls me Danielito."

"Can I call you Danielito, too?"

"Of course!"

"What country were you born in, Danielito?"

"Peru, Don Fernando."

•　　　•　　　•

His bright eyes sparkled with glee, lending a special glow to his baby face. Danielito and his little sister had come to New York with their parents from Callao, Peru's main port city, a dynamic, lively place. In Callao they lived in a poor but relatively peaceful neighborhood where his father worked as a fisherman and his mother, like so many other women, did needlework and sewing to make ends meet. She had learned how to make tapestries out of fabric scraps, and the money she earned went toward meat, clothing, and shoes for the family.

Nevertheless, they had heard so many stories about the limitless opportunities in the United States, and they began to dream of a better life for themselves and for their children. Finally they decided to risk everything to achieve this dream. Their first few years in New York, however, were difficult, and things didn't turn out so well for them. They eked out a living in one of the poorest areas of the Bronx, and were constantly at each other's throats over their economic hardships and all the other difficulties that all immigrants go through. Daniel's father worked scrubbing the floors and bathrooms of a Chinese restaurant, and his mother cleaned houses for Hispanic families. In New York, the little boy no longer received the attention he had grown accustomed to, and as if that weren't enough, he had had to witness the disintegration of his parents' marriage. The intense pressure they both felt often exploded into bitter arguments, physical abuse, and, finally, separation.

Before coming to New York, Danielito had grown up like so many other Latin American children, with a relative amount of freedom but always surrounded by family, grandparents, uncles, aunts, and cousins. In New York, he spent a lot of time alone, locked up in their apartment reading science fiction and fantasy novels, dreading the moment his parents would return from work. Any encounter between the two easily and often degenerated into a fight.

When they told him he would have a big brother, he lit up with anticipation, anxious to meet him. At home there was no one he could talk to about all the things that fascinated him, like science and art. Every time his father found him reading, he scolded his son for bothering with "all that nonsense" and told him he ought to study something "useful," like auto mechanics.

Fernando looked him in the eye before asking the question:

"Are you hungry?"

"Yes, sir, very, very hungry."

"Well, let's go down to the little restaurant downstairs. It's my treat. You can leave your backpack here, in the closet. I promise it'll be safe."

The little boy did exactly as he was told. Standing just a few feet away from him, Fernando observed his movements, thinking hard about what he could do to be a positive influence on the young boy's life. Watching as the little boy obeyed his instructions, the brand-new big brother thought about all the dangers lurking out there for a little boy like Danielito, like his nephews and niece, all of them so young. Silently he gave thanks for the chance to be a part of his life.

Together they left the office, united by a charitable organization established back in 1902 by an employee of the Children's Court of New York.

"Hey, don't leave me behind, son, I can't keep up with you!"

As he watched Danielito skip down Roosevelt Avenue, Fernando remembered what the program coordinator had told him about Danielito when he called up to confirm his participation. He could hardly imagine how frustrating it must have been to witness his parents' conflicts, and he was glad to hear that Danielito had found some kind of refuge in books.

"This is a smart kid who loves to read. Maybe you can help him, take him to the library, or do some book-related activity," suggested Triana, the program coordinator.

Food first, thought Fernando, for whom eating was a great source of pleasure and comfort. He himself had already enjoyed a massive breakfast to help calm his jangled nerves after the very stressful coordination of a young boy's funeral, a nine-year-old just like Danielito. In the space of twenty-four hours, he had said good-bye to one child and welcomed another into his life. For that reason, it made sense that his niece and nephews were on his mind at the moment. But right now he had to focus on his lunch guest.

"Let's see, Danielito, what would you like to eat?"

"Meat, rice, beans, oooh, they have shrimp! My mother says shrimp here are really expensive . . . I like them so much, Don Fernando, can I order some?"

"Are you sure you're going to have enough appetite for all that?"

"Oh, yes!" he chirped, opening his eyes wide, as if the question was superfluous.

"Well, all right, go ahead . . ."

"Thank you, Don Fernando, you're so nice!"

"It's a pleasure to eat lunch with you, Danielito."

It takes so little to make a child happy, thought Fernando. The simplest little sign that he or she is important to you, listening and responding to what they say—those are the things that really matter. Communication between the two "brothers" was on the right track.

The little boy proceeded to order, and asked the waiter to give him the food on the "biggestest" plate they had. The word made Fernando laugh, and immediately he, too, asked for a similarly large portion. As they sat there, eating their meal together, Fernando thought about how he hadn't enjoyed anything like this since the last time he'd taken his sister's kids out for lunch.

"I hope you don't get sick on me, with all that food you're planning on putting away!"

"Are you kidding?" the child exclaimed, shrugging. "Whenever we had enough food, I always used to say, 'Mommy says I'm a bottomless pit!' But it's been a long, long time since I ate like this."

The comment made Fernando's heart ache, and he had to hold back his tears from the sudden wave of emotion. He could almost hear his own mother right then, admonishing him and his siblings for not eating everything on their plates when so many children in the world went hungry.

"Well, I want you to fill up, and good, but don't go getting sick, because your teacher wouldn't like you to miss out on school."

"I promise, Don Fernando, I've got plenty of room for the food I ordered."

Fernando gave him a couple of pats on the shoulder, and then asked:

"Do all the kids in Peru eat that well?"

"In my country we eat even more, the food in Peru is so good. . . . You know, you'd be even fatter if you lived there." As soon as he said it, he realized he'd stuck his foot in his mouth. "Please, I didn't mean that, it wasn't right to say that . . ."

"Don't give it another thought, Danielito. I've been overweight for years and I know it. We're brothers, and brothers don't need to go around worrying about things like that. But I'm afraid you're not going to be able to finish what you started to eat; you're going to look like one of those little chickens that they fatten up with corn."

"Oh, wow, you know, I think I forgot to order the chicken."

"Are you serious?"

The instant the food arrived, Danielito stopped talking—his mouth was busy with other things. Without rushing, but at the same time totally focused on the task at hand, he concentrated exclusively on savoring each and every bite until finally, the plate was clean as a pin. He looked up and smiled.

"That was such a good meal, Don Fernando. Thank you so much."

"Sure. If you don't mind, I'm going to order a coffee."

"Of course not, go right ahead, enjoy."

•   •   •

After finishing the coffee, Fernando paid the bill and took Danielito on a visit to the public library. The little boy, thrilled, began to clap with delight. Once inside, they inquired about getting library cards, and after filling out the applications and receiving their cards, they went over to the children's section. Daniel picked out a book to read that week: the first book in the world-famous saga by J. K. Rowling, *Harry Potter and the Sorcerer's Stone.*

"Today we have initiated a brotherhood that I hope will unite us for the rest of our lives. But we also share a responsibility: this library card allows us to take out a book every time we see each other. But we have to return it in perfect shape. Deal?"

"Today has been such a great day, Don Fernando. Thank you so much for being my big brother."

He gave Fernando a big hug and then put the book in his backpack.

Just as he had promised Mr. Triana, at six-thirty Fernando met Teresa, Danielito's mother, at the entrance to the Roosevelt Avenue subway stop. They greeted each other warmly, and as he shook the woman's hand she looked him in the eye and said:

"You are a guardian angel."

"Thank you, ma'am. I know we'll be seeing a lot of each other. You know where to find me if you ever need me."

Saying thank you over and over again, Danielito hugged his new big brother. Holding hands, mother and son climbed the stairs to the train. When they reached the top they turned around to wave good-bye one last time before entering the station.

As he got ready for bed, Fernando replayed the afternoon he had shared with his new "little brother" and couldn't help but think back to the other children who had passed through his life. He had known many in his day, some in quite precarious situations, little boys and girls living through circumstances that would mark them for the rest of their lives. He always asked himself, every time, how it was possible that parents didn't think about their children before getting involved in illegal activities. He could never forget the tremendous anguish and abandonment he had seen in so many children's faces.

One of the cases that had affected him the most was the case of little Clara. The despair and desolation he saw in her eyes would always be somewhat bittersweet. Far older than her years, Clara de los Milagros was sent to him, he was convinced, by the Christ of Monserrate, much venerated and prayed to in Colombia. Fernando, in turn, entrusted the little child to him, and he made a miracle happen—one of those miracles that nobody ever hears about or talks about because they happen every day. One of those miracles that anybody could help carry out if he were simply willing to be the vehicle to make it happen.

According to what the neighbors told him, the little girl hiding behind her mother's skirt had witnessed the violent treatment her father had received from the police before he finally broke down and showed them the place where he had stored the five kilos of pure cocaine they knew he had hidden. There it was: inside the mattress upon which the little girl, Clarita de los Milagros, slept every night. When he heard about what had happened, via a telephone call, Fernando put his network of connections to work. He searched for information about the girl's family in Colombia, sought out official help in Jackson Heights to get her handed over right away, and hoped to avoid any investigations if possible.

When he arrived at the police station, he kissed the little girl on the forehead and identified himself as her mother's cousin. Clarita didn't even react to this, and everyone present simply assumed that she was still in a state of shock after all that she had been through. Fernando took advantage of the moment to explain to the authorities that what the little girl needed most was to return to an environment where she felt comfortable, with her family. He told them that he had already spoken to her grandparents, who were now waiting for her in Colombia.

Thanks to his connections, in half an hour Fernando managed to get temporary custody of the child and a safe conduct so that she could travel. As soon as the documents were issued, he and the little girl left the station hand in hand. In Clarita's free hand, she clung to a pink Barbie suitcase.

While Fernando took care of these details, he asked one of his employees, Giovanni, to buy a ticket for the first flight leaving from New York that arrived in any city in Colombia. They had to act as quickly as possible, because the government officials might try to stop them.

Fernando, Giovanni, and Clara took a taxi to John F. Kennedy International Airport. During the half-hour ride there, Fernando told the little girl who he was and explained what they were trying to do: get her back to Colombia so that her grandparents and her aunts and uncles could take care of her. As she listened to him, Clara looked into his eyes and Fernando suddenly saw that her eyes were a deep shade of green, the color of clouded hope.

He offered her candy he'd bought at the little store a few steps away from Fernando Travel, but all she wanted was a little bottle of apple juice: "My mommy always buys me one when we go out for a walk," she stated, making herself heard for the very first time.

"Listen, we're going to make a plan for this trip that's going to get you back to Colombia, where everyone is waiting for you so they can give you a big hug."

"I miss my grandmother and my cousins, we used to play at their house all the time."

"Just you wait, you're going to play with them again real soon, I promise."

"Where are my parents?"

"They're taking care of some legal problems."

"Is my daddy sick?"

"No, sweetheart, he's sad because you've been crying so much."

"I was so scared."

"He knows that, and he's very sorry that all this had to happen."

"I didn't know about those white bags inside my bed. What do they use them for?"

"Honey, try to forget everything you saw, it's not good to think about those things."

They were just reaching the airport when his cell phone started ringing. He had a bad feeling about who was calling. After studying the number that appeared on the readout, he picked up, and sure enough, he heard the nervous tone of voice of a federal agent informing him that they couldn't authorize Clarita's departure.

"But what do you mean? Everything's in place. Her grandparents are waiting for her to come off the Avianca flight that's leaving here in three hours."

"Impossible. We can't allow it. We'll be there in about twenty-five minutes to pick Clarita up. The traffic is awful right now."

"Well, all right, we'll be waiting for you," Fernando said. He would have to put their emergency plan into action. Thinking on his feet, he quickly hung up and started phoning his contacts inside and outside the airport.

Little Clarita listened to all the conversations, looking up at him all the while, her eyes filled with questions. After giving another one of his colleagues a series of instructions, he turned around, looked at the little girl, and said to her:

"Listen, sweetheart, there's been a change of plans. The game we're playing to get you back with your grandparents is going to be even more fun."

The little girl listened intently, not missing a single detail, and promised Fernando she would follow his instructions to the letter. When they finally reached the airport, they hurried out of the taxi.

"So do you think you'll be able to do just what I told you to do?"

"Whatever you say. Here's my Barbie suitcase. You'll take care of it, won't you?"

Once inside the airport, they got down to business. First they presented the safe conduct to the agent at the check-in counter, who confirmed its authenticity and validity. After they left the ticket counter, they waited a bit, and before long they caught sight of two agents dressed in the typical outfits of plainclothes policemen—the kind of clothes policemen wear when they don't want to seem "official." The men smiled when they saw Fernando with Clarita, who was standing next to a boy that Fernando introduced as Giovanni.

"All clear for us to take her?"

"Yes . . . well, I wanted to call Clarita's grandparents so that Clarita could talk to them before you leave with her."

"Can you do it quickly?"

"Of course, of course."

The little girl looked at him from the corner of her eye. On the loudspeakers, they heard the last call for the Aeropostal flight to Quito. Right then the pink suitcase fell to the floor with a thud and Clarita started squealing.

"What's the matter with her?" one of the agents asked.

"Honey, what's wrong?" asked Fernando, a concerned look on his face.

"I have to go to the bathroom, I need to go pee-pee . . . pee-pee, pee-pee," she wailed, and started to cry.

Fernando turned around to look at the agents, and asked them to let her go to the bathroom. Giovanni would keep an eye on the ladies' room door. In the meantime, Fernando needed them to sign a document that he had in an envelope but that he couldn't seem to find. His search for the elusive slip of paper dragged on for some ten minutes until one of the agents finally asked how far the bathroom was. Was Clarita all right?

They all began walking toward the bathrooms, which

were located just opposite the boarding gate for the flight to Quito. Moments before, Clarita had entered that gate, clutching the hand of an Aeropostal stewardess who Fernando had arranged to sneak her on the plane.

"It's the first time she's ever traveled alone and she's a little bit scared," Giovanni told the stewardess, kissing her on the cheek. Then he looked at the little girl and said,

"Don't you worry, Clarita, your grandparents are waiting for you, and this lady here will look after you on the plane."

Following the sudden disappearance of Giovanni and Clarita, Fernando asked the federal police to launch an investigation:

"Maybe some drug trafficker was following them and kidnapped them!"

As soon as Clarita arrived in Colombia, her family sent a thank-you note to Fernando. Her parents are still in jail. Just as he had promised, Fernando sent the pink Barbie suitcase to Clarita, along with a new Barbie doll and a pink blanket "so that you'll remember me, your friend from New York, whenever it gets cold." He never forgot that tiny girl from the Colombian coast with the pained eyes, the same little girl he prays for every night, asking her guardian angel to look after her.

Every Christmas he receives a card with her photo that he places in his family photo album. Clarita is now a lovely young woman whose education he takes care of from his office in Jackson Heights.

•   •   •

Meeting Danielito brought back all these memories. In order to devote the time he felt the boy needed from him, he squeezed a few extra hours out of his weekly schedule so that he could see him almost every Saturday afternoon. At least twice a month the "brothers" went to the public library, where they picked out all sorts of fantasy and science fiction books: Ray Bradbury, William Gibson, J.R.R. Tolkien, Edgar Rice Burroughs, Ursula Le Guin, Lewis Carroll, C. S. Lewis, Isaac Asimov, and many others. As the years went by, Danielito entered high school, and his already considerable curiosity flourished. He began expanding his literary horizons, reading more and more books by experimental writers.

One day, when he was a teenager, Danielito invited Fernando to a lecture by William Gibson, one of the main figures in the cyberpunk movement. Fernando could hardly believe it. The kids—and this included Danielito—showed up for the event wearing such outrageous clothes that Fernando thought he might faint. But in the interest of maintaining his relationship with his adopted brother, who was navigating through the treacherous waters of adolescence, he kept his cool. Still, it was like going to a meeting of extraterrestrials where, without a doubt, he was the odd man out, and looked it.

"Breathe normally, these people don't bite," Danielito whispered in his ear, amused.

"Are you sure?"

"I give you my cyberpunk word . . ."

"Listen, I have to ask: has something happened to you? Is there some problem you don't feel comfortable telling me about?"

"No, nothing. If there was, I'd tell you, I promise. You're my brother."

"Don't you forget it."

Danielito continued to immerse himself in the world of cyberpunk, following the footsteps of writers like William Gibson, whom he idolized. In his typically honest manner, Fernando told him that he'd rather hang back in the more familiar territory of witches, or else in Hogwarts with magician's apprentices like Harry Potter and his friends. And though Danielito continued to expand his repertoire of literary tastes, books have always remained a particularly special point of communication for the two brothers.

During life's trickier moments, Fernando and Danielito have always been able to find a way of connecting with each other, and to discuss painful subjects from a more global perspective thanks to the books they have read. They have been able to confront personal issues with a distance that allows them to truly respect each other's point of view.

When Danielito was in his second year of high school, his English teacher asked the class to write an essay about an especially meaningful moment in their lives.

Danielito, now known as Danny, decided to tell the story of something that had happened to him years earlier: "It was a sunny day," he wrote, "and it was still very cold outside when Mommy told me to wash up good and put on my best clothes . . ."

That, of course, was the day she had dropped her son off at Fernando Travel, where Danny met the best brother in the world. The teacher was impressed by the boy's writing style, and recommended him to a number of writing programs. She also urged him to join a writing workshop for teenagers.

"I would never be the person I am now. I would never be on my way to study literature at Brown University, I would never have read all that I have read, listened to the music I have listened to, I never would have gone to the opera, or to the Metropolitan Museum of Art, where I saw a pyramid for the first time. I still remember how I couldn't believe my eyes, a pyramid in the middle of Manhattan. All thanks to the man who came into my life to be my big brother. My big brother, Fernando Padrón. Thank you . . ."

With those words, Danny graduated from high school, with the highest grade point average in his class: a young Peruvian boy who was now a full-fledged American citizen. He spoke and wrote perfect English, and in his spare time he worked as a tutor for disadvantaged kids. With the money he earned, he had been able to save enough to buy his mother a sewing machine. Once again she was able to make the tapestries she loved to create. And as for Fernando, Danny bought him a leather-bound date book with an inscription in gold that read: "My big brother: FP."

Danny, the son he'd never had, the boy whom God had placed in his hands as his adopted brother, was now in his sophomore year in college, getting excellent grades. During his summer vacation, Danny spent a couple of weeks helping out at Fernando Travel, getting the computers up to speed. That was Danny: the same Danny who had recently introduced him to his girlfriend, a beautiful young woman named Lillian. A girl who had the same kind of joyful face as Danny, filled with hope and optimism. Both of them were certain that the future was full of great things.

Life continued to smile upon them. And then, one day, a pink-colored envelope that smelled like fresh violets arrived at Fernando's office. It was from Clara de los Milagros. Inside, a fetching young woman in her twenties from the coastal city of Barranquilla smiled at him, with both her eyes and her lips. In her arms was a beautiful newborn baby, wrapped up in a pink blanket that he recognized instantly. In the letter the proud mother invited Fernando to visit Colombia to attend the baby's baptism.

For these and for so many other reasons, Fernando called Big Brothers and asked Mr. Triana to find him another little brother to adopt. The terms were the same as before: every Saturday he would see the child in his office, so that he might dedicate the best hours of his day to him. His work was important, Fernando realized, but the effect his love and concern could have on a child was incalculable. He was willing to do whatever it took to reach as many kids as possible.

In the meantime, of course, he continued solving the problems of all those who sat down at the other side of his desk. The line of men and women only grew longer and longer every day.

For Danielito, the wait had been worth it.

8

November 13: Adrián and the Angels

Fernando saw him again during one of those thundershowers that seem like a prelude to the Apocalypse: it poured harder and harder until it felt like the end of the world was upon him. An intense, icy rain that transported him back to those winter mornings in the coffee-plantation region of Armero, a place of sweeping contrasts filled with gunslingers who waited out the afternoons, sitting quietly at their doors. One could sense the specter of violence in the family nucleus inside their homes.

Those hit men, snot-nosed adolescents who in many cases were barely of legal age, sat with blankets over their legs to cover the Uzis they always kept close at hand. They were on guard, ready to fight at any given moment.

Firmly entrenched in his work chair, where he directed rescue operations from Jackson Heights to Colombia, Fernando idly wondered what had made him think of Armero and those hit men. At that moment, his eyes came to rest on the calendar: November 13. Of course. Now he understood why pain suddenly yanked at his heart, the pain of the country, *his* country. He lit a cigarette and watched the rain fall; it was one of those rare moments he was alone, when silence reigned supreme in his storefront. All he could hear was water sliding down the gutters and crashing in torrents against the pavement in a nearby alley. It was as if the rain was giving the neighborhood a good cleaning. It could use it, he thought. In fact the neighborhood, the city, the country, the continent, could all use a cleaning to wash them free of the pain they lived with.

He prepared some coffee to go with his cigarette. Though he didn't smoke much, he always liked to feel how the coffee's flavor blended with the taste of the cigarette. He inhaled each puff with depth and pleasure, like a young kid playing with smoke rings, dreaming up a dream for each one he exhaled. Engrossed in contemplating the inside of one of these smoke spirals, he noticed a figure pressing against the window. Yet everything was blurry, and he couldn't make anything out very clearly. As he narrowed his eyes to focus, the figure began banging against the windowpane. He didn't think it was a client but he went over to the door anyway.

The human being he found standing at the door to his office assaulted his nasal passages with a bitter smell that jibed perfectly with his tattered appearance and the forlorn blue eyes that seemed to have sunk into a reddish well.

"Sir, please, won't you give me some money to get something to eat?" asked a hoarse voice that sounded tremendously familiar to Fernando, a voice that bore an inflection that brought him back to the same coffee plantations he had been thinking of just a few minutes earlier.

It wasn't hard for Fernando to understand what dire straits this man was in; he was soaked to the bone, and his clothes clung to his thin body, making his already impoverished image appear more so. Fernando politely ushered the man in, turning aside to let him past.

"Just let me rest a little bit inside here, the cold and . . . oh, the angels, they're after me. I promise not to take much of your time, sir, it's just that I'm exhausted and you see, the pain in my leg is just about unbearable," he said, collapsing onto a pair of plastic cartons full of clothes. They had been delivered from a plant in New Jersey that was closing up. In the following weeks, Fernando's mother would be distributing them among people in need.

"If you could just give me a little bit of money for some soup, I'd be so grateful," he said, looking around with the empty gaze of a man who couldn't see, and then he shook his arms as if trying to shush someone. "I'm just exhausted, you see? I want to go back to Colombia to rest, and to get away from all this sadness."

"Colombia? I knew your accent sounded familiar. We're from the same place, man."

"I'm leaving, I'm leaving!" the man said in an alarmed voice, trying to get on his feet. "You're one of those angels that's after me, day and night you're after me."

Before the man could get all the way up, Fernando stopped him, handing him a cup of coffee.

"Here, have some coffee and wait until the rain lets up."

The man burst into tears.

"What's the matter?"

"Oh, it's been so long since anyone's served me a cup of coffee like that . . . just like my mother used to, before . . . a long, long time ago."

"Isn't it nice to enjoy a cup of coffee with the rain coming down outside?"

After the man gulped down his coffee, he looked up at his host, implored him for another cup, and Fernando obliged. The man drank the second cup as fast as he had consumed the first, and when he was done he tried to smile, but the effort resulted in a pained grimace. Fernando responded with the warmth for which he was famous. Before sitting down, he said, "You know, I think it's going to be a while before the rain lets up. I'm going to call the joint on the corner and order a couple of soups. What do you say?"

"I would say thank you for being generous enough to treat me like a human being."

"Well, isn't that what you are? A human being?"

"Oh, you can't imagine how I feel when they look at me and treat me as if I were some kind of criminal, which I'm not and never will be."

"Cheer up. Life puts some tough obstacles in our way precisely so that we can overcome them."

"Mine have been too tough."

"Let me go and call in the delivery, and we can talk about all those obstacles while we wait for the food to come. How does that sound?"

"I think you're the kind of angel that doesn't intimidate me."

Fernando smiled beatifically as he walked over to the phone on his desk. When he returned, he placed a chair just a few feet away from the homeless man, looked him in the eyes, offered him his hand, and said,

"My name is Fernando. And yours is . . . ?"

The man's eyes blinked rapidly as he responded:

"Someone I loved very much was named Fernando, but I haven't seen him since . . . a long time ago. My name is Adrián, Adrián Linares."

Trying to control his own rapidly blinking eyes, Fernando looked in the pocket of his plaid shirt for the leather cigarette case that had once belonged to his grandfather, and offered it to Adrián. Both men lit cigarettes and said nothing for a few moments, enough time for Fernando to recover from the impact of hearing the poor man's name, enough time to walk down memory lane to Colombia, all the way back to that sunny afternoon when, on one of his first trips back home, he had decided to visit Armero. He had been standing on a street corner wondering which way to go to find the hotel where he would be staying, and had turned to a stocky young man around his age and asked him how to get there. The man walked him to the door of the establishment, and just before they parted, Fernando reached into his pocket to offer him some money. The gentleman's response warmed his heart:

"No, my friend, I haven't done anything to earn your money. If you'd like we can have a cup of coffee, that would be more than enough."

As they drank the coffee, they shared their stories. The young man, whose name was Adrián Linares, confessed that he dreamed of going to America to escape the violence that plagued them on the streets of their small town. He wanted to escape the terrible fear he felt for his family, especially his sister, so young and so pretty. That first coffee together led to another and another and even a few breakfasts as well, during which time the young man asked Fernando everything he could think of about the city he dreamed of moving to someday. Finally, the moment arrived when the two men went their separate ways: Fernando to Medellín en route to New York, and Adrián to his daydreams. Adrián took down Fernando's address and promised to write him, but no letter ever made it to his office. Fernando figured the young man had never achieved his goal. But then again, maybe he had. After all, he'd done it.

Lost in their thoughts, the two men remained silent for a few more minutes until someone yanked them back into the present moment: it was the deliveryman, ringing the buzzer to hand over two generous portions of soup, accompanied by slices of bread that the two men devoured without a word. When they finished, Fernando prepared another pot of coffee, not mentioning the fact that he'd recognized the homeless man. He simply poured the coffee, offered him another cigarette, and invited Adrián Linares to tell him the story of how he had come to New York.

At eighteen years of age, Adrián Linares left Colombia. Between the drug trafficking and the guerrillas, life had become impossible. If you escaped one group, you fell into the clutches of another. After the U.S. embassy denied him a visa on three separate occasions, he decided that his only chance to get to the destination he so desired was by way of the coyotes.

Of course, it may have looked like a coincidence, but it wasn't: as he walked out of the embassy, a stranger stopped him and asked him why he was so troubled, and Adrián told him. This generous young man led him to a ramshackle office down an alley in Armero and introduced him to Elkin, who offered him two possible ways to get to the United States: plan A, by plane with fake visas; or plan B, the "brave man's path," by plane from Colombia to Nicaragua and then to Phoenix, Arizona, on foot. Unaware of the dangers, he felt drawn to the promise of untold adventures in the second plan. He could sell his motorcycle. That would cover part of the price, and he could earn the rest pretty easily, by delivering some packages, the contents of which were unknown to him. Plan B cost four thousand dollars up front and six IOUs for three hundred dollars each, which he would begin to pay forty-five days after arriving at his destination. It was a deal.

He didn't regret placing his life in such danger, but he did feel badly about leaving home without saying a word to his good mother. He couldn't tell her where he was going, and prepare her for the aching desperation and the pain-filled days that would follow. He just left. It took him forty-five days to cross Central America—all the way from Nicaragua to Phoenix on a path fraught with peril, where hundreds of his countrymen had lost and would continue to lose their lives. To make it across safely he had had to assume a new identity, and he soon became José Antonio de Izapán, a Mexican. Along with six other people who were also trying to get into the United States, he reached Bogotá, led by an associate of Elkin's who taught them what they needed to know in order to pass themselves off as Mexicans: the national anthem, the food, the accent, certain slang phrases, the currency, photos of different places in Mexico.

They warned the men that the trip would be brutal, and that they would have to learn to be tough if they wanted to survive. After a few classes, he was given a passport with his photo, under the name of José Antonio de Izapán, with a visa (he never knew if it was real or not) for Nicaragua and an airline ticket on a Nicaraguan airline with a connection in Costa Rica. He was traveling light, with just three changes of clothes and a wad of money, around a hundred dollars.

Everything that Elkin warned them about came true. In Costa Rica the authorities held and examined them from head to toe, turning their socks inside out, practically ripping the soles off their shoes in search of drugs that none of them carried. And as much as they begged for a decent hotel where they could sit out the bad weather, the policeman with the withering gaze just threw each of them a pillow and a blanket and pointed to the floor of the airport, which was where they spent the rainy night until the following day, when they left for Nicaragua. The immigration officers at the Nicaraguan border told them that they knew their visas were fake and the men had to swear over and over again that they were real before the officers were convinced.

They then headed for the city, where an individual

wearing the red baseball cap with the word CAMPEÓN emblazoned across the front never showed up to meet them as they were told he would. In desperation they called Bogotá, where they were told to go to a location without a street address: first, three hundred steps toward the lake, then two hundred steps past the old bakery, then they were to cross the street where the old movie theater was. No street names, no numbers. They were positive they had been cheated, but the taxi driver who picked them up knew exactly where to take them—a dirt-poor neighborhood somewhere in the capital.

They knocked on the door of the house where the taxi driver dropped them off and were greeted by a couple who silently ushered them inside and informed them that they wouldn't be able to go back out onto the street until nighttime. At that point another taxi took them to a different neighborhood that, hard as it was to imagine, was even more impoverished than the first one. They spent two days locked up in a creepy house where all they could do was sit around and play cards. Every time they wanted to call their families in Bogotá, they were charged five dollars. Adrián's one decent memory from those dismal days was the first hot meal he was given: plantains and refried beans.

At several points in the story Adrián had to pause, breaking down in tears, unable to go on. Fernando could only watch, feeling terrible about the horrible experiences that thousands of people had had to live through to achieve their goals. Among his compatriots, the dream of making it to the promised land often drove them to embark on dangerous adventures that, in many cases, ended up costing them their lives.

The first coyote finally appeared and introduced himself by saying,

"I'm Manolo. Get moving, it's time to get started." He was barely twenty, but his ruthless manner made him seem decades older. He looked at them as if they were a flock of sheep and then ordered them to reduce their already tiny bags to no bigger than a soccer ball. Everyone tossed out the contents of their backpacks, holding on to only the most essential items, and followed him. By the time they got on the bus to Honduras it was dark, and by the time they arrived they were tired, hungry, and frightened.

The odyssey, however, was only just beginning: the darkest moments were still to come. The rain was coming down in buckets, just as it was outside of Fernando Travel that night, and it was pitch-black outside when the bus stopped and they were told to climb onto the back part of a double-traction pickup truck that was waiting for them. Under these conditions they made their way through the jungle.

When they reached the end of the access road, they jumped out of the pickup truck. The coyote reminded them that they would have to walk ahead of him, and that under no circumstances were they to stop for anybody. Anyone who stayed behind would be left to fend for himself. It was about nine P.M. when they began walking, one behind the other. Adrián could barely see the man in front of him, the same man whose hand he was hanging on to for dear life. A tree branch scraped against his pants leg and broke the skin on his thigh. Without even flinching, he kept on walking.

He was just about ready to collapse when a bright light off in the distance suddenly jolted the somber procession back to life. The coyote calmed them down, telling them not to get scared, and not to talk, move, or cough until he gave them orders to continue on.

Finally, they reached a pickup truck, the source of the lights. They all went into the back part of the truck, and the coyotes covered them with a canvas dropcloth, to make the vehicle look like a military supply unit. They traveled for a long, long time before they finally came to a stop and heard the coyote say,

"All right. Get out."

They did and followed him to a building on what looked like an abandoned plantation in the middle of the jungle. From there they were led to a hut with stone floors and a roof made of palm leaves. The nine Colombians were left there alone. The coyotes walked away, warning them not to leave the shack—as if any of them, after all they had been through, would have felt intrepid or inspired enough to start exploring the local terrain.

Despite the cold, the men fell asleep on the freezing floor, without blankets or anything else to keep them warm. When they woke up the next day, the coyotes brought them what would be their menu for the weeks to come: tortillas and beans. They stayed in the hut for three days. Blessed was the rain that fell down on them, for it allowed them to wash off and clean some of their clothes.

"I'm going to be your guide," announced another man after the very long wait. His name was also Manolo, and he was very young, just like the previous coyote. He was walking them over to a rickety bus, when, out of nowhere, the first Manolo reappeared in the middle of the road, and said,

"Listen, there's a problem. I need you to lend me a thousand dollars."

What other choice did they have? Fading out into the shadows, Manolo II promised to return at eleven P.M.

By three A.M. nobody had returned, and the group had begun to sleep in shifts, to avoid getting caught by surprise by a military troop or a police unit. They were certain that this was it, that it was all over, when suddenly they spied a large vehicle that turned out to be a packed bus, with the coyote up front. The nine men climbed onto the bus, barely squeezing in. That dawn they entered Guatemala. Without a word, Manolo II paid back the loan—not out of honesty but out of deference to the law of the jungle. He knew that if he didn't make good on his promise the other coyotes would slit his throat.

Adrián paused and asked for another coffee to give him enough strength to get through the rest of his story. As he drank the contents down in one gulp, he shivered, looking out the window, as if he'd sensed a bad omen on the horizon. Suddenly he stood up, as if he were about to leave. Though the rain wasn't coming down so hard anymore, it hadn't let up, either. Fernando pointed this out softly:

"Why don't we keep talking, at least until the rain stops? It won't be much longer."

"To look at you, anyone would think you're actually interested in my story!"

"Of course I am, Adrián. Tell me the rest of it, whenever you're ready . . ."

The homeless man smiled enigmatically and eased back down into his chair, sipping the few drops of coffee left in his cup. He closed his eyes for a short while, and when he opened them, he continued on as if he had never stopped talking.

Their road for the following six hours was a dried-up riverbed. The thirty-nine men and women on this adventurous expedition, for lack of a better term, held on to one another by the hand, as if they were on a kindergarten field trip. When they finally reached Guatemala City, the group split apart, and he and a friend headed for a hotel the men in Bogotá had told them to go to. They remained there for five days, and were actually able to sleep in a bed and walk around the city in relative peace.

Their rest ended, however, with the arrival of Manolo III, a Colombian who told them that in a little while they would receive Mexican identity cards. He gave them all the information they would need: names, addresses, places of birth, where they went to school, and other details. Manolo then told the men that in Mexico they were to speak to him and only him.

At the border, they slept in one of several shacks that was filled with Latin Americans. Some had been there for weeks, others for months, waiting for their families to finish making the payments for their passage across the border. The place was total chaos: the walls were covered with messages, and the people were all piled on top of one another, sleeping on the floor. Each little shack was outfitted with an improvised candlelit altar where people prayed constantly for the miracle that would allow them to cross the border with a coyote.

Gracias a Dios—"Thank God"—was the name of the

border town where Adrián and a large group of Latin Americans embarked for Mexico. After a twelve-hour walk, they climbed onto an old, heaving bus filled with local farmworkers. In the middle of the ride, a police car stopped the bus to make an inspection. Adrián was sure that they were going to be arrested—anyone could see that they were illegals from a mile off, but luckily as the passengers had started talking, a bond of solidarity had formed, and the farmworkers quickly exchanged clothes and handed over their animals so that the people in Adrián's group looked like Mexicans.

From the spot where the bus dropped them off, they could see a hill off in the distance with some scattered posts here and there: Mexican territory. It was already night when they started walking, and by the time they began to wade their way into a river, it was so dark that Adrián wondered out loud,

"How am I going to cross if I can't see anything?"

Manolo III told him what to do.

"If you want, you can just stay behind."

Adrián continued advancing through the river, using a fallen tree to help guide himself across. Suddenly a girl clinging to the tree began to cry,

"I can't! I can't!"

They never saw her again. After crossing the river, they arrived at a little cabin where they were given watery soup before stretching out to go to sleep. Nobody knew where they were, and nobody asked. As they slept they could feel something moving across the floor, tiny little feet scampering over their bodies. They were so exhausted, though, that they couldn't do anything but give themselves up to God and cover their faces to protect themselves from the rats that ran from one end of the granary to the other.

A few hours later, the coyotes woke them up, shouting, "Get up, you're in Mexico now!"

Manolo handed each of them one thousand Mexican pesos and put them in separate taxis headed for Mérida, the capital of the Yucatán. After all they had seen and visited, this was, without a doubt, the first pretty place Adrián had laid eyes on. And some kind of miracle must have occurred, because they were then told that they would be staying there for five days, in a hotel that was just like paradise, with comfortable beds, clean bathrooms, and with plenty of time to get to know the center and the outskirts of that lovely city. Manolo III's tour of duty ended there in Mérida, and as he bid the men farewell he handed them their Mexican documents and plane tickets.

They made sure to wear very clean clothes for the flight: first to Mexico City, and then on to Chihuahua. They would be traveling in small groups of two to three people, and the coyote gave them extremely precise directions about what to do and where to go, down to their departure gate. Just after landing in Chihuahua, they were getting ready to leave the airport when they were stopped by the police.

"Where are you from?" he asked.

"Mérida," he said, and the policeman just nodded and indicated which way to go.

When he arrived at Chihuahua's Plaza de Armas, the city's main square, Adrián was stunned by how much it resembled the architecture in Bogotá, and he felt a twinge of sadness as he thought of his family. There in the plaza, he waited for an hour, but nobody came to pick him up. Nervous, he called Elkin and explained that he had gotten separated from the group.

"What are you wearing?" Elkin asked. Adrián told him and Elkin told him to go over to the tortilla stand next to the church. Before hanging up, he promised Adrián:

"Don't worry, in half an hour they're going to pick you up there."

Half an hour later a black taxicab pulled up in front of him.

"Adrián?" Two young Mexicans called out from inside the cab, smiling at him. "Get in, brother, come on in with us."

They hadn't gone two blocks when the younger of the two said, "Hey, man, give us a little something for gas."

After handing them a few pesos, Adrián was delivered to a hotel where his Colombian companions were waiting for him. As soon as they mentioned that they were part of Manolo's group, the hotel made room for them.

That night, they got onto a bus that took them out to the desert, where a van was waiting for them. From there, they drove for hours and hours through vast dunes, which never seemed to end. Inside the vehicle they were protected from the cold, biting wind, but the van had no heat, and the raw air penetrated their bones, leaving their hands and feet numb.

"You don't know what you've got until it's gone," Adrián later said to himself. The van was paradise compared to what they would endure when they were ordered to get out and start walking. They obeyed, doubled over, often falling down, without anyone around to come to their aid. They walked for hours and hours. Their nerves frayed, their skin cracked, their bodies exhausted, and their hands and feet frozen, the only thing that kept them going was the hope of reaching their goal. Adrián never figured out exactly how long it took them to walk through that desert, but it felt like an eternity. Suddenly, almost out of nowhere, a massive hangar appeared before their eyes a short distance away. When they reached it, a tall, burly man dressed in dark blue overalls called out to them:

"Welcome to the United States, amigos!"

Overcome by emotion and fatigue, they all fell to the ground. They were then given bowls of hot canned soup that tasted absolutely delicious. Hours later, they were herded into another van, where, once again, they felt the icy chill of the desert whistle through the canvas cloth that covered them.

Their next stop was a gas station, where a Mexican gave them a warm welcome:

"So, what do you think of the United States?"

He then told them to get into a van with seats and heating, and brought them to a Wal-Mart to buy a change of clothes. They had to go in two at a time; otherwise they would have looked like a pack of criminals just released from hell itself. Then they were brought to a covered area where they were hosed down, to remove the dirt and grime that had accumulated on their bodies over the previous few days. Scrubbed clean, well dressed, and their hair combed, they took off for the airport in Phoenix, Arizona. There, Manolo IV said hello and good-bye to the nine Colombians as he handed them their airline tickets, but not without first giving them a postal address to which they were to remit payment for the plane ticket.

"Yours," he said to Adrián, "cost $270. You can pay me back at this address. Send it by Western Union."

The nine men, companions and survivors of this misbegotten adventure, embraced one another and wished one another luck before heading off on their separate paths. Adrián's flight brought him to New York, where, forty-five days after leaving Bogotá, he finally arrived at John F. Kennedy International Airport. As soon as he reached Manhattan he called Doña Mercedes, his mother, whom he tearfully promised to help as soon as he started to earn some money. And that is exactly what he did.

With a heavy heart, and without another word, Adrián got up and walked toward the door. Fernando tried to stop him, but by the time he had grabbed his coat to go out to Roosevelt Avenue, Adrián Linares had already disappeared.

Several weeks went by, and Fernando glumly accepted the fact that he had lost Adrián for a second time. But then, one Sunday morning when he was in his office organizing his papers, paying bills, and solving all the things he hadn't been able to take care of during the week, he felt someone staring at him. Looking up from his work, he saw a figure pressed up against the front door, his eyes focused on some distant place that did not seem to be situated within the real world. Fernando rushed to open the door and let him in.

"I just put up some coffee," he said. "Sit down and have a cup. Then we can order a real breakfast from the joint on the corner."

Adrián entered and stopped in the middle of the little

office. His face illuminated, he announced in a thunderous voice,

"There's no escape, they're going to come after us soon . . ."

"Who?" inquired Fernando.

"The angels will come first, to prepare the way for the lady."

"What lady?"

Fernando could see the delirium swirling round and round in his pupils.

"The virgin who will announce the end of New York, just like she did in Armero."

"Were you in Colombia when everything happened in Armero?"

"I didn't get there in time, but I should have been there to stop the end from coming . . ."

Adrián began to cry inconsolably. Fernando pushed him a tiny bit, to get him into a chair, and gave him a bit of water to sip. As was his habit, it seemed, Adrián drank it down in one gulp. Little by little he calmed down, settling into a kind of daze. He remained like that for a while.

Suddenly he stood up, looked at Fernando, and smiled.

"What's your name?"

"My name is Fernando. We met a few weeks ago. You came to visit me, don't you remember? Why don't you drink some of your coffee?" Fernando said, indicating the cup that he had placed on the folding table next to the plastic cartons located in the same place they had been the first time Adrián had come by; Doña Lucrecia still hadn't found the time to separate all the clothes and deliver them to the organizations that helped those in need. Adrián drank down the contents of the coffee cup; then, when he was finished, he placed the cup back on the table.

"The other day you told me about how you made it to the United States, but you left before finishing the story. Where did you go when you first got to New York?"

Adrián nodded his head.

"Would you mind pouring me another cup of coffee?"

Once again Fernando filled the cup. As if catapulted by a spring, Adrián launched right back into his story, reliving the trip that brought him to New York. Don Padrón, like the impromptu confessor he often was, settled into his chair, close to Adrián, and listened.

For the first few months following his arrival, Adrián lived with friends and acquaintances, and even got himself a job at a restaurant in the East Village. He knew he'd be able to earn a living as a cook without too much trouble, and since he needed to pay off his debt to Elkin, send money to his family, and find a place to live, he began working. He would start in the early dawn as a cleaning boy, first washing everything down and then getting the restaurant in tiptop shape. At midmorning he changed duties and became the cook's assistant, who quickly took note of his abilities and began letting him season certain dishes with Latin-American flourishes, to add a little spice to the menu. It soon proved to be a great success: the dishes Adrián doctored up became very popular, and the cook began allowing him to add more and more variety to the restaurant's offerings as time went by.

Adrián had learned these recipes from watching his mother and his sister María Clemencia prepare meals at home. They were the source behind this initial impulse, a point of departure for combining his instincts with what he had learned at home, and he turned this endeavor into an art. His idiosyncratic method of preparing shellfish, drenched in flavor, came straight from the culinary traditions of his mother country, straight from the kitchen of his mother and sister. He began writing to them, and with every letter he learned a new secret; the letters they exchanged were like master classes in cooking, giving him a reason to feel very, very proud.

With each experiment he learned more and more. Little by little he made a name for himself, earning respect in the restaurant kitchen at first, then among the customers, and as time went by, in the restaurant business at large. His amazing talent for seasoning and preparing sauces reflected a deep knowledge of and sensitivity for ingredients, textures, and flavors, and a willingness to take risks by blending ingredients that were unusual and exotic.

Adrián smiled when he reached this part of the story: he, Adrián Linares, had been the pioneer of those culinary innovations. In addition to his talents as a cook, he also had a special aesthetic gift when it came to the presentation of his dishes.

Adrián rose through the ranks, unstoppable. The restaurant promoted him to assistant chef, and a few months later he was offered a considerable salary to join the legendary team of the kitchen at the Four Seasons. That was when his star began to rise for real, as a cook who was well on his way to becoming a celebrity chef. The Four Seasons took good care of him to make sure he didn't get lured away by some other restaurant. He was such a valuable asset. His name alone drew customers, and his bank account reflected his incredible professional ascent. One day, one of his bosses showed him a review that someone had written about one of his culinary creations, and from then on, his name began to appear regularly in newspaper and magazine columns about the most interesting innovations in the local dining scene. Critics and customers adored meeting him because he was a simple, guileless person who was so clearly passionate about his chosen craft.

Fernando was shocked to learn that this helpless, homeless soul sitting before him had once been a celebrity.

At first, Adrián said, he felt panic at the thought of having to go out and greet people, having to say hello to the customers in his rudimentary English, but things slowly changed as his self-confidence improved. First, he began taking English classes, and years later he actually gave classes about incorporating Latin-American elements into Continental cuisine. The kitchen had become his mode of expression, the place where he could release his emotions through dishes.

As he earned more and more prestige and money, he was able to make one very special dream come true: he bought a house for his mother, the kind of house that she had always wanted, with her own bedroom and separate bedrooms for all her children, including him, "for when you come home, my son," and for the grandchildren "who hopefully will come one day." It also had a spacious, luminous kitchen filled with appliances that his mother had never even heard of, much less dreamed she would ever own. And a television with a giant screen, "so you can really enjoy your soap operas, Mamá."

He also hired a woman to live in the house, to clean, do the shopping, and take care of everything else because he didn't want Doña Mercedes to have to work another day in her life.

"You've worked enough, Mamá," he said to her over and over again. She lovingly chided him for the never-ending stream of gifts he regaled her with.

Despite all the fame, the time away, and the distance from his country, Adrián kept the promise he had made to his mother when he first arrived in New York. Whether close to home or far away, his mother and sister were his number one priority. He dreamed of bringing them to live in New York one day, but they loved Colombia, and they were terrified by the idea of such a big city and all the dangers people said lurked there. Whenever they said that, Adrián just laughed: the danger was back there, at home, not in New York!

Adrián stood up and began rummaging through the pockets of his ratty jacket. After extracting a half-filled flask, a sandwich wrapped up in a napkin, and a piece of chocolate, he pulled out a scrap of newspaper which he carefully unfolded and, still standing, handed to Fernando:

"Here you are, sir, so you can see I didn't make any of that up." Something in Adrián's thick voice conveyed a kind of equanimity, as if a tremendous sense of peace had come over him.

The newspaper clipping included a photograph of an attractive, dapper man, along with a tiny bit of small print. There was Adrián, dressed in a well-tailored jacket, looking straight into the camera with a smile on his face. Above the article you could make out the *New York Times* logo. It was Adrián, no doubt, just without the beard and the tatters, much younger, and far more lucid-looking than he was now. Just as he had done the first time, Adrián turned around, raised the lapel of his jacket, said good-bye, and walked out, closing the door behind him. Once again, Fernando rushed around in search of his overcoat. He found it under a pile of folders on a desk at the back of the office, but by the time he had made it out onto Roosevelt Avenue, Adrián was nowhere to be found.

For two whole months, Fernando berated himself for getting so caught up in Adrián's storytelling that he hadn't thought to ask where he lived, or how he could help him out. He was furious at himself for having lost him again— that is, until Adrián reappeared, as was his habit, on a day when Fernando was all alone in his office.

This time around, Adrián looked a bit less haggard, and the jacket he wore wasn't quite as destroyed as the previous one. His stench, though, was every bit as stifling: as he greeted Adrián, Fernando felt a wave of nausea come over him, and had to make a serious effort to hide his involuntary response to the fetid odor emanating from the man's body. Afterward, when Adrián left, he opened the doors wide and lit incense to air the place out and get rid of the awful smell.

Right then, however, he focused his attentions on the man who looked him in the eye and informed him of the following:

"I've come to say good-bye. The angels are coming to take me with them, to be with María Clemencia again. She told me that everything there is nice and calm, that I'll like it there. Finally I'm going to see her again."

"Where is María Clemencia, Adrián?"

"In heaven, with Mamá . . ."

"How did they get there?" Fernando asked, surprised by what he had just heard. Until then, he had assumed that Adrián's family was still in Colombia.

As if he instinctively knew all the questions running through Fernando's mind, Adrián sat down in the same place he had the other two times, next to the plastic cartons that were beginning to become permanent fixtures in the office. Fernando handed him a cup of coffee and, as was his habit, Adrián drank it down in one gulp before he began talking.

To speed up the process of becoming a U.S. citizen, so he could bring his family into the country, Adrián had married an older woman, a friend of one of his bosses who had agreed to help him out. They became very close friends during the two years they lived together, but once he received his green card, they got a divorce, out of mutual accord. Adrián admitted to Fernando that his ex-wife was very worried about him, and had tried to convince him to find a doctor who might help him through his many troubles. She couldn't accept that the only thing he wanted in the world was to be reunited with his mother and sister.

Ten years had gone by since he'd left home, and as soon as he received his green card he applied for citizenship and prepared to visit his mother and sister in Armero. After requesting a month off from work at the restaurant, he went out to buy gifts in the little boutiques up and down Third and Fifth Avenues, at Saks Fifth Avenue, Bergdorf Goodman, and Barneys. His sister had gotten married and had had children, and so he also bought bags full of toys at the legendary toy store FAO Schwarz.

On November 13, 1985, a taxi carried him and his four suitcases, stuffed to the gills, to JFK airport—the very same airport where he had arrived ten years earlier. As excited as a little child, he boarded the Avianca plane. For the duration of the flight, all he could think about was getting home, imagining the surprised faces of his mother, María Clemencia, his brother-in-law, and his nieces and nephews when they saw him walk through the door. He was sure that when Panchín, his dog, sniffed him from a distance, he would jump with joy and run straight into his arms.

Adrián had arranged for a rental car, and planned to travel around the country with his family, something his mother had always dreamed of doing. Well, now he would make that dream come true. He could scarcely contain his jubilation.

From high up in the air, he looked down on Bogotá and the surrounding landscape, and thanked God for all the blessings he had received. When he arrived at Bogotá, however, an unnerving surprise awaited him at the airport. The first thing he noticed was that the airport staff and the police looked exhausted, and he felt a strange, inexplicable anguish hanging in the air. But it wasn't until he walked over to one of the newsstands that he found out. He thought he might explode from the pain and shock: on the front pages of all the newspapers were the most gruesome photographs of people who were dead, or wounded, unspeakably horrific images. The headlines were blood-curdling: WIPED OFF THE FACE OF THE EARTH, said one. THE WORST TRAGEDY OF OUR TIME, said another. Finally, on the front page of *El Tiempo*, he read, HORROR IN THE WAKE OF THE NEVADO DEL RUIZ ERUPTION.

An eruption at Nevado del Ruiz? He quickly paid for one of the newspapers and raced through the article on the front page. That was how he found out that a powerful mud slide had destroyed the town of Armero. He walked over to a policeman. What had happened? The policeman's chagrin said it all:

"Oh, sir, it's been just awful. Everyone in Armero is dead."

Suddenly he felt as though the entire world had collapsed, and that he had remained outside, stunned, and buried in the most excruciating solitude. Everything he loved in life was gone, and there was no way he would ever get any of it back.

Somehow he managed to get to the outskirts of the town, where he found Doña Griselda, one of his mother's close friends, who hugged him as if he were her own child. All dead, she told him. An indescribable pain tore through him from limb to limb. Ever since then, he was plagued by the sensation that dark angels were following him everywhere he went. But María Clemencia had finally sent her people to get him, so that they could once again be together as a family. Forever.

Adrián returned to Bogotá and went straight to the U.S. embassy, where they phoned his restaurant. The woman he had married flew to Colombia and brought him back to

New York, but he never recovered from the blow. He had been wandering around New York for about a year with those dark angels dogging him at every turn.

"I can't even bury them; they never found the bodies. Trapped in the mud. And ever since then it's as if I've been trapped in the mud, too. But now the angels are going to take me to see my mother . . ."

Fernando moved closer to Adrián, but before he could give him a pat on the arm Adrián said,

"I came to say good-bye to you. You've been so kind to me. May I ask you for a coffee so that we can toast our friendship, sir?"

"I'll get some ready right now, it won't take a second."

He didn't even feel it as the door closed behind the man in tatters. But when he returned with the two cups of coffee, he knew Adrián had gone. He scolded himself one last time for letting him go.

This time he knew he wouldn't see Adrián again, and he cried long, slow tears of frustration and pain.

9
Lucy

The sun shone down hard, as it does on those winter days when it seems as if the cold has scrubbed the world clean, and the sun's rays have dressed up in their finest clothes. On this day, the fierce, incessant wind howled through the air, penetrating even the heaviest of overcoats. The frigid air whistled through the layers of clothing that everyone wore—coat, jackets, sweater, shirts—and settled into the pores, assaulting the skin until it shivered uncontrollably.

Unable to see the beauty in any of this, Londoño asked himself why on earth he had ever left the island that he once called home.

"Who the hell told me to leave Puerto Rico for the god-damn arctic streets of a working-class neighborhood in New York City?"

Some twenty cars had converged on the quiet road in the residential section of Jackson Heights. The doors opened and some fifteen policemen wearing bulletproof vests and carrying automatic weapons ran toward the modest two-story house.

Curtains were drawn on the windows of the house's second-floor master bedroom. The police now had the place surrounded. Her back to the street, Lucy looked at herself in the mirror. The woman who looked back at her had little or nothing in common with the girl she had been only a few weeks earlier. Had her mother seen her like that, she would have crossed herself and prayed for her daughter's soul.

On her feet were the most expensive shoes she had ever worn. In her handbag, which matched her shoes, she placed an envelope. She had never even dreamed she would own shoes and a bag that actually matched: up until a few months ago she had only one pair of cheap shoes which she wore all the time, and a backpack where she kept her most essential possessions. She looked in the mirror: what she saw was a Lucy who didn't look a bit like the person she really was.

That morning, as per Braulio's orders, she was to deliver the money to the customs agents so that they would look the other way when the drug shipments came in. She was risking a lot, paying a very high price in exchange for nothing: she wasn't free, she wasn't happy, her mother was far away and there was no one she felt she could trust. Not one single friend.

Lucy's original plan was to swallow the capsules, make the trip, receive the payment, and return home so that she and her mother could open up a little business. She was young and naïve, though, and she hadn't managed the situation very well: she never should have started talking to Braulio when he came by to meet the new mules. Not only did she talk to him, but she told him the story of her life— about her mother, her problems, and then she made the huge mistake of accepting his offer to take her out to dinner. She didn't have experience with men; that was her problem.

"I'm stupid, so stupid, the stupidest person in the world, that's what you are, Lucy Santa María. You should have gotten out when you had the chance. You shouldn't have given in, but you did, you gave in, you gave in. You should never have accepted these rags, but you did, here you are. I shouldn't have turned into this. I don't want to be this woman, I don't want to, sweet God, Señor de Monserrate. God, oh God, please help me get out of this somehow!"

That was the moment when she heard the cries:

"Lucy, Lucy, get into the hallway!" It was the voice of Darío Rengifo. "Shit, Lucy, run . . . look for the exit door . . . run!"

She went out to the hallway and felt the bullets smash against the walls, the windows, and everything else that was in her path.

Darío clambered up the stairs with a mini Uzi hanging from his shoulder, his right hand holding on to the handle so that pulling the trigger would be a cinch if it came to that. As the bullets pierced the windows, broken glass went flying into the thick fabric of the curtains. Lucy barely managed to remove her high heels before she went running like a bat out of hell down the second-floor hallway. As the bullets perforated the walls, slivers of sunlight started to dance around the inside of the house.

Behind Darío, Juan and Zacarías fired away. A bright red explosion was all Zacarías managed to see as a bullet blew his head open: a bright red explosion that spattered the walls. At that point, Lucy was only a few steps away from the door that led to the secret tunnel that Braulio Rentaría had decided to build. It had been finished just a few weeks earlier by the workers brought in from Colombia. The little passageway had two exits, one that led to the street in front of the house, and another one two blocks away.

Desperate, Lucy raced to the door, behind which she could hear the sound of police officers screaming,

"The woman! The woman! Don't let her escape!"

She had never been so panicked in all her life. After she opened the door she spun around and saw Darío lying on the ground, wounded in the arm but still firing away toward the stairs. Next to him lay Juan, dead, his body ripped open with bullets. She shut the door behind her and locked it with the bulletproof metal reinforcement that had been installed so recently.

Her feet sliced up from the broken glass, she made her way down the tunnel. She knew there was no way out through the door that led to the street opposite the house because the police would be waiting there for her. Trembling, she advanced in the darkness until she reached the other exit, convinced that she would rather die than go on living like this.

"This is it," she said to herself. "This is my chance to escape the police and Braulio."

It wouldn't be quite as easy as she hoped.

With a harsh expression and flinty eyes, Detective Londoño hiked up his coat collar, adjusted his hat and gloves, grabbed the thermal mug filled with steaming coffee, got out of the car, and headed to his office. Finally! On his desk, fourteen days after issuing the request, he found a thick folder filled with reports on the most elusive mules in the business, the kind that the police rarely managed to get their hands on.

Each of the nine case files on his desk contained the classic drug mule story: the poor young man or woman who had gotten involved in the business of using his or her body to transport drugs, and now lived on the run from drug lords and the police. One by one he went through the files: Manuel Ronceros, Peruvian; Felipe Gallo, Argentinian; Silvia Rojas, Colombian; Teresina Requena, Colombian; Graciela Picón, Colombian; Reyes Salas, Colombian. He flipped through the files, and then spat out a few profanities. All of them were over thirty, and the women were all dark-skinned.

In a typical gesture of disgust and hostility, he slammed the sheaf of papers down on his desk. These people weren't anything like the girl they were looking for, not in the least: according to the reports, she was no older than twenty, of medium height, had blondish hair, and was impossible to miss because she looked just like a doll. None of those photographs even remotely resembled that description.

He stormed out of his office, bitching and cursing, and barged into the office of Gil, the investigator in charge of cases involving missing mules. At this point Londoño was so enraged that he was no longer a man; he was a wild beast and didn't bother to hide his frustration and fury.

"Gil!" he barked. "Do you think I'm going to settle for this kind of shit?"

"But, chief, I gave you the files first thing in the morning, and—"

"The girl we're looking for isn't here! Or perhaps you're confabulating with her, could that be it, Gil? Tell me!"

"What does that mean, chief, 'confabulate'?" asked Gil, trying to buy himself some time. He knew that Londoño was a frustrated professor.

"Oh, so you don't know your ABCs, either? *Confabulate*, Gil, *confabulate*, it means to go around conspiring with someone. Now that you understand the word, maybe you'll give me a straight answer."

"Your comment is offensive, chief, and I think it's uncalled for."

"We're looking for a twenty-year-old blonde and you're sending me files filled with a bunch of old hags!"

Seeing his boss this furious, Gil knew that it would be a waste of time to even try arguing with him. When Londoño got that way the best thing to do was just let it go; he'd calm down in a little while. "He's going to retire soon anyway," Gil thought, not even bothering to look up. "Better just let him be and wait until he calms down."

Londoño paced back and forth in Gil's office like a caged tiger. He was looking for someone to fight with, just to let off some of the steam that had been building up inside of him. He didn't have much of a chance, though, because Gil barely looked up at him; he was too busy studying the documents Londoño had thrown at him. Three yelps later, he left Gil's office, slamming the door behind him so powerfully that the walls shook.

He walked outside and glanced down at his watch. The case had him unglued, but part of his agitation stemmed from the disgruntlement he had been feeling almost all the time. He'd lost track of how many years he'd been alone, without any friends, always doubting himself. His parents were long dead, and he had no contact with his family in Puerto Rico. He felt exiled from the world, and it had been a long, long time since he'd experienced a triumph in his professional life. When was he going to get a break?

To defuse his frustration, he decided to dive into his work. As he walked toward Roosevelt Avenue, he resolved to spend the rest of the afternoon interviewing people and taking notes on every last detail he could uncover about that mysterious woman who had slipped from their grasp a few hours earlier. They had come so close when they surrounded that mafioso's safe house. For years Londoño had been trying to get his hands on something, some piece of information that would finally allow him to arrest Braulio Rentaría, but no. Nothing. At least they had managed to catch Darío Rengifo, Rentaría's right-hand man. Darío could have escaped, but they had managed to catch him because he had stayed back so that the elusive mule could get away. Despite everything, the guy was a brave sonofabitch.

Inside the house, not long after the gunfight with automatic weapons had ended, shots of another kind rang out in the air. Microphone in hand, Leyla Sonora smoothed out her hair and the camera panned across the disaster scene. They were ready to go on air, reporting from where the policemen had been wounded and the criminals had been arrested. Leyla opened with a brief introduction on Darío Rengifo, known for being the mafia chief's second-in-command, the most important figure among those arrested.

With her index finger, Leyla guided her TV audience over the bullet holes in the walls and across the blood-soaked floor. Then she led her cameraman up a flight of stairs to the room where, only minutes before, Lucy had been preparing to flee. There, Leyla found an unexpected source of inspiration:

"Cut! What on earth is this?" As she surveyed the closet, Leyla couldn't believe her eyes. "Where did all this clothing come from? These shoes? These pocketbooks? Oh, are we ever going to show the world how these mafiosos treat their favorite mules. . . . This is unbelievable." She prepared to go back on camera. "Attention, everyone . . . We are interrupting our regular programming with a special report, live and on location . . ."

Not far away, in a hermetically sealed safe house, Braulio Rentaría watched the TV news report, smoking a cigarette from his third pack that day. All he could feel was rage as he watched Darío, his closest confidant, emerge wounded and handcuffed from what used to be his home. The bile rose as he watched Leyla Sonora smugly announce the death of Juan, and his emotions turned into seething fury when he saw her rooting through Lucy's room. She revealed all sorts of private things, showing her clothes, her bags, her shoes, and other gifts he had given her. But Rentaría really lost control when he saw Leyla grab and open the small pocketbook that had been tossed onto the bed. The camera zoomed in on the inside of the purse, which contained checks from a false company made out to the names of several customs agents: the checks that Lucy was supposed to have delivered personally. How the hell could she have left that bag behind? Why hadn't she brought it with her? All his customs contacts that had taken him years to build came crashing down with that one camera shot. He would never forgive that reporter. Never.

"Goddamn bitch," he said, stroking his beloved silver-plated Smith & Wesson, his favorite weapon. He never went anywhere without it. "Enjoy your little moment of glory while you can, you fucking cunt," he growled. "Enjoy it because you don't have much time left. I swear to you, Leyla Sonora, there's a bullet with your name on it."

Watching the news report from the little TV set in his office, Fernando sighed deeply and wondered if Leyla hadn't gone too far this time. He was worried about her. He'd never said so directly, but he was fond of her. He liked her style, her persistence.

• • •

Gun in hand, Rentaría dialed a number and yelled into the phone:

"Did you find her? Did you find her?" Without waiting for a response, he spat into the receiver: "You better get hold of her, wherever the hell she is. Don't make me go out and do it myself because then I won't need you people anymore. Do I make myself clear?"

He slammed the phone down so violently that it crashed to the floor and split in two.

"That's what I'm gonna do to Leyla Sonora."

Lucy's freedom didn't last long: in less than twenty-four hours, the thugs sent out by Braulio picked her up without a problem. They had a solid network of informers all over Jackson Heights who quickly told the boss's men where to find her. And they found her, despite the fact that she was somewhat disguised by the rags that a homeless woman had given her in exchange for the clothes she'd been wearing when she escaped.

She was sitting next to a trash-can bonfire when two of Rentaría's men walked over to her, grabbed her by the arms, one on either side, and dragged her over to the car they had parked in a nearby alley. She didn't even put up a fight; she knew that protesting would only make things worse.

In a short while she was standing in front of the man who treated her as if he owned her. She wondered if she would ever be able to escape his clutches, he was so powerful. Her head felt as if it were about to explode, between the aches and pains from the cold she had caught and the lecture Rentaría was giving her for having left the purse with the checks on the bed. All she wanted was to run, run away from everything. Run and run and keep on running until she reached Colombia, to her house, to her mother.

Braulio kept on yelling at her:

"... *Pendeja!*" he snarled, pacing from one side of the room to the other, glaring at her with fury in his eyes. "I suppose you realize that the police have us by the balls now that they found your bag with those checks. You realize, don't you, that thanks to your little oversight we're all about to get thrown in the can, you stupid bitch?"

"I didn't do it on purpose," Lucy said, trying to explain her actions, and began to cry. "It all happened so fast, Darío started to shout, the police were already inside—"

"Shut up, goddammit, and stop your squealing! The damage is done and I demand payback."

"But what can I do for you now?" she pleaded.

"A lot, my darling. A lot. You, as Lucy, are of no use to me anymore. You killed Lucy when you failed us out there. Right now I need you to be my bait with the cops. I'm gonna stick you into the wolf's mouth, baby, a wolf that's getting too close to me, but he'll never be able to resist your charms."

"But they all must know who I am, they must have a file on me . . ." she said, frightened.

"They know you from behind. They've never seen your face," he said, turning around to yell at his thugs. "Get me a pair of scissors! Scissors, goddammit, or didn't I say it loud enough?"

Lucy quickly tried to cover her hair, but it was useless. Rentaría made a lunge for her, and while two goons held her down, he chopped off her hair. Neither her sobs nor her trembling, delicate body could stop him.

"Take her and . . . dye her hair black, or something, I don't care what color," spat Rentaría.

Lucy glared at him with hatred in her eyes as they dragged her out of the office. A couple of hours later they returned with a much-altered Lucy.

"Now, I am not going to say this to you twice," he warned in a thundering voice. "For starters, let me remind you that Lucy no longer exists. From now on your name is Tania Castellanos. Your IDs are ready. Everything's all set. You're going to go to work as a whore on Roosevelt Avenue. Once you get there, your mission is to get yourself shacked up with that fucking investigator who's on our ass. We need you to get as much information as you can out of him. The guy is sharp, a little unsociable, but you'll be able to soften him up all right. As for us, I don't have to tell you: not one single word about us, otherwise we're gonna send your pretty little head as a gift to your mama in Colombia."

"What's the cop's name?" Lucy asked, still sobbing.

"Jack Londoño, the sonofabitch. Memorize it, baby: Jack Londoño."

A few nights after Rengifo was placed in police custody, Londoño went out on a night shift to get some leads on the mule who had disappeared. He went into a local nightclub, the Chibcha, and ran into Roberto Mestanza, also known as "El Pencho." A Puerto Rican who sold information to whoever paid the most for it, El Pencho surprised him that night with the following tidbit:

"Hey, chief, you can call off the investigation on that

chick everyone's looking for. They told me she came off the Colombia flight last Tuesday. They say her face turned up on the airport security video."

Londoño raised his eyebrow.

"Pencho, I came here to talk business with you and you give me that shit? Don't you think we've already looked at those videos over and over and over again? Where the hell's your instinct?"

"Chief, man, the info is for real," said Pencho.

"You're lucky I don't have you locked up for being an asshole," Londoño said with a sneer.

Never one to break habit, Londoño emerged from the club cursing and bitching to himself. Then he drove over to police headquarters, got out, and climbed the stairs to the imaging department. Two minutes later he was scanning the video taken the previous Tuesday at JFK airport, scrutinizing every single frame, backwards and forward. Pause and rewind. Pause and rewind.

Suddenly, around minute 23, something caught his eye. Painstakingly he slowed the video down so that he could see it second by second. In the far left-hand portion of the screen he spotted a girl: medium height, dark blond curls that reached her shoulders, a long black coat covering her legs down to her ankles. From the side, not allowing the camera to catch her face-on, she approached a customs agent and spoke to him briefly. Blurry image. Rewind. He couldn't tell if she had given him something or if they were just talking. Seconds later, without inspecting her luggage, the agent walked her over to the exit.

The woman had made it through as free as a little dove; nobody laid a finger on any of her things!

As if jolted by an electric shock, Londoño jumped up and went over to his computer to check if, on that day, Tuesday, February 22, some foreign dignitary had arrived in New York, someone who would have received special treatment. Nobody.

He looked at his watch: it was almost four in the morning. He jumped into his car and drove over to the Chibcha. By then, the only ones left there were a few hardcore regulars. Londoño looked around for Pencho, but he was nowhere to be found. In a couple of easy chairs nearby, a few young girls nodded off.

He sat down on one of the barstools and ordered a rum. Then, quite unexpectedly, he felt someone's fingers brush against his shoulder. He didn't know it right then, but when he turned around, his life would change forever. All he would remember was how his heart raced when he came face-to-face with those immense, deep eyes, the kind that had the power to make time stand still. He felt a fire ignite inside him when she asked, "Buy me a soda?" Her childlike face seemed tired.

"A soda?" Londoño smiled. "I would have thought you'd be drinking something else. Where are you from, anyway? I've never seen you around here before."

"I'm just getting started. I used to work across town, but I came here because my friends told me the customers were better. Do you come around here often?"

"No," replied the policeman, who couldn't take his eyes off her for a second as he shouted over to the bartender, "Harry! Give the lady a soda!" Then he said to her, "I come whenever I can—"

"To work," she interrupted him. "You're a cop, aren't you?"

He didn't reply.

He looked her up and down; she was a real beauty, no doubt about it. She wore her black hair short, and on her thin, well-shaped body she had a tight, baby-blue dress that left her delicate shoulders and long, slender arms bare. As Londoño watched her stand up and reach over him to get her soda, she seemed tiny, defenseless, fragile. She told him she was from Bogotá and that she was twenty-six years old, but Londoño had the feeling she was a lot younger and just said that to avoid getting in trouble with the cops. He didn't say anything, though, and he remained quiet as she told him about her life back home, of her job picking bananas for the United Fruit Company, her illegal journey into the United States, and her rapid entry into the world in which he had found her. The hours went by like seconds.

"Oh, my God, it's eight in the morning!" she said, surprising herself.

"Well, don't go disappearing on me like Cinderella, sweetheart. At least tell me your name."

"Tania. Tania Castellanos."

"Can I see you again sometime, Tania? Or actually, if you'll let me, I'll take you wherever you want to go." She looked at him with tired eyes.

"I'm sorry, but I'm too tired to work now . . ."

The look on Londoño's face as he gazed at her was so unbelievably tender that nobody he knew would have ever recognized him.

"I don't want you to work, Tania. I just want us to be friends."

"All my friends are back in Colombia," she said wistfully. "Oh, it would be so nice to have a friend here. Thank you . . . what did you say your name was?"

"Jack Londoño, at your service."

"Thank you, Jack, but I have some things to take care of inside."

With that, Tania disappeared into the back of the club, not realizing that she had forever changed the lonely life of Jack Londoño.

"I want to work for you," she said, wrapping herself around his chest.

Londoño held his breath and gently pushed her away. Whenever her skin made contact with his, a strange and marvelous sensation ran through his body, unlike anything he'd ever experienced before.

There was no way he could maintain his resolve with that face, those eyes looking at him like that. But something inside of him told him to wait, to be a tiny bit prudent, not to get too involved too soon. That something, though, was becoming vaguer and vaguer with every passing moment. His better judgment was slipping away, and soon it would disappear entirely.

"I don't want you to work for me, Tania."

She moved closer to him and whispered in his ear,

"Jack, what I mean is that I want to work for you for the rest of my life."

Londoño couldn't resist the invitation that he had desired from the very moment Tania had asked him for a soda, there in the Chibcha, in that baby-blue dress, with those bare shoulders. As his mouth traveled across her body . . . shoulders, arms, legs . . . that body, so fragile to the eye, drew him in like a powerful net, plunging him into a world that he had avoided for so long.

As her body brushed against his, everything suddenly became unbearably urgent, an uncontrollable desire, a drive that was pure and total surrender, a torrent of blood that boiled furiously as the fragile-looking woman traveled over his thighs, his belly. As she slowly, expertly explored him, he discovered signs of life in parts of his body that he had long since given up for dead. As Tania revived them, they became hers; she became the absolute mistress of his body. Their passionate embrace was the kind of surrender that opened the doors to heaven itself, uniting them forever. A song of hope in the middle of all the excrement and filth that they had been forced to live through.

Three days after Pencho gave him the information about the airport video, Londoño finally located him again, sacked out in a bar on Ditmars Boulevard after one too many lines of cocaine.

"Hey, *pendejo*, who gave you the info about the airport video?"

"Chill out, chief, don't freak out on me!" Pencho replied, annoyed. "There's no way I can tell you, man, because I don't know the guy who gave me the info."

"Pencho, don't be a fucking bastard, or else I'll haul you in for refusing to cooperate with the police."

"No, I'm serious, chief. The kid sat down at the bar,

drank a couple of drinks, and started to sing. He said that the mule all the cops are looking for is right under their noses. And if you'll excuse me for saying so, chief, he said that all you guys were a bunch of idiots for not realizing—"

"Well, who is the sonofabitch?" asked Londoño, about to lose what little patience he had.

"I told you, I don't know!"

"Well, you better go and find out. You've got twenty-four hours. Otherwise I'm reserving a room for you in jail. Got it?"

Londoño started up his car and headed out to Rikers Island; Darío Rengifo would be waiting for him at the prison. A mafia conspirator and one of the last men arrested by the police, Rengifo had agreed to cooperate with the police in exchange for his family's protection. He was absolutely critical to the investigation.

"The key to moving those last shipments was the girl," he told Londoño. The boss brought her in the minute he laid eyes on her. She's real refined-looking, and seems like such a quiet little nothing. The boss thought she would be the perfect person to move around from place to place. Nobody would ever suspect her of anything. She went through customs, made all the contacts, brought the money, delivered the messages, she did everything. And, of course, the boss made her his girlfriend, but he made sure never to load her up with too much money because he was always afraid that one day she'd start talking and leave him."

"Why did she leave, then, if she had everything going for her?" asked Londoño.

"Come on, man, you know what chicks are like. She

was always going around moping and crying all the time because she missed her mommy, because she wasn't in love with the boss. She's scared to death of him."

"What's the girl's name?"

"Lucy. Lucy Santa María."

10

Against the Odds

Spring was in the air: you could feel it, and you could see it as people turned up the collars of their light jackets and strolled beneath the trees that would soon come alive with baby green leaves. At that hour of the night, of course, most people in the neighborhood were in bed. The next day they would all have to get up early to leave children at school before heading off to the factory or office.

Londoño, however, had eyes for only two things that spring season: the elusive mule they still hadn't managed to locate or identify, and his beloved Tania.

On this particular Tuesday night at 9:30 P.M., Londoño,

too impatient to wait for the elevator, ran down the stairs from his apartment and out to his car, parked on the street. He could feel his heart racing just as if he were a teenager rushing out to see his very first sweetheart, and not the man of forty-eight that he was.

He burst out laughing when he stopped to think about it: it was true, he had fallen in love just like a teenager, as if Tania were the first woman he'd ever been with. As he pondered this, an unusually joyful glow came over him. Maybe she wasn't the first, but she was definitely the one who had gotten under his skin, more than any other woman.

Two months after they met at the Chibcha Club, Jack and Tania continued to see each other every Tuesday evening. Yes, maybe the arrangement was a bit strange, but it didn't faze Jack, who lived in a world where strange was the common denominator. One thing that was crystal clear to him, though, was the love he felt for Tania, a love that had changed him so profoundly that when he woke up in the morning and looked at himself as he shaved, he had to ask himself how it had all happened. He couldn't quite believe it was all true.

As part of the many professional rituals he observed, Londoño continued goading Pencho, trying to get more details out of him about that airport video. That, after all, was the reason Londoño had gone to the Chibcha in the first place some two months earlier. Ever since that early dawn visit, of course, he now traveled to the club with a very different name dancing in his mind, a woman's name: Tania Castellanos.

Sweet Tania's tenderness and sensuality had won him

over and turned him into a sentimental, sensitive soul. For reasons he didn't quite understand, they could see each other only on Tuesdays. This logically became the most wonderful day of the week for the veteran investigator who, oddly enough, never thought to investigate the person sitting right under his nose.

He had already spent time with Pencho, trying to get him to cough up some more information about the person behind the airport video tip. In reality, though, when all was said and done, the information didn't mean that much to him anymore. His purpose in that bar had one name and one name only: Tania. His greatest pleasure was simply watching her, talking to her, and catching a glimpse of her eyes, such impossibly lovely eyes. He felt overcome with anxiety when he didn't find her there, and felt, quite literally, stung by a piercing sense of jealousy when he sensed that her professional pursuits were the reason for her absence. When she was there sitting at the bar, though, life became something else entirely.

The most trivial conversations had a way of transforming their little world into an island in the middle of all the madness around them. He loved hearing her laugh as she told him about her life on the banana plantations, about the Sundays she spent in the kitchen with her mother, making *sancocho de gallina*, with delicious aromas swirling all around them. And when it was his turn to talk, his stories transported them to the heavenly beaches of the island of Puerto Rico—his one and only pleasant memory from childhood.

"I want to see you, Tania. Always," he said that first night, holding her hands tightly.

She smiled. From that day forward they agreed to meet every Tuesday, no matter what. It was a pact they sealed; there was no escaping it. They had fallen in love, into that vertigo that rises up from the soul. She asked him for only one thing in exchange for that wonderful dream: that they never talk about the present.

"Leave the present," Londoño said. "Leave it behind and come with me to live in the future."

But that was more than Tania could hope for. Why had life delivered her such cruel blows? How would she ever escape that nightmarish labyrinth and finally be free again? How could she sweep away all the mistakes she had made?

"One day, Jack. One day," Tania whispered in his ear, trying to control the tears that threatened to spill from her eyes. As she leaned her head against the chest of the one man she truly loved, he tenderly stroked her hair. With all the energy she could summon, she concentrated on never forgetting that moment, so that it would remain with her forever; she would hold on to it like a prayer for those moments when the worst was upon her.

Leyla Sonora was walking on air, more than ever before. The news report she had delivered from the bullet-pocked house had catapulted her into another dimension. In the Latino news world, she was, without a doubt, the most renowned, most adored, and most respected journalist because she didn't just deliver the news—she delivered justice. Her audience ratings had skyrocketed, placing her far ahead of the competition. Thanks to her soaring fame, Leyla's pretty face and bright red hair were now the centerpiece of the TV station's new ad campaign. Microphone in hand, Leyla Sonora smiled out at the city from taxicabs, subway platforms, and bus shelters. She was everywhere, riding high on a wave of success, and she didn't plan on letting go of any of it for a long, long time.

Plus, she had only scratched the surface of the juicy Jackson Heights mafia. She was sure of it, ever since someone tipped her off about the existence of a photo of the mule that everyone was looking for. Leyla was determined to get her hands on it. With that in mind, she primped and preened even more than usual before her appointment with Detective Jack Londoño, because she did not intend to leave his office until she had that magical photo in her hands. She looked in the mirror: yes, yes, she really did look dynamite. But was all this fuss worth the effort? For that man who barely ever looked at her, much less flirted with her? Did he even *like* women?

"Jack, why are you always so mean to me? You always say you aren't around when I know perfectly well that you're working in your office."

"Leyla Sonora, I have nothing to share with you," he answered brusquely.

"Come on, I've cooled off these last few days because I know you've been busy, but we all know about the explosive material you're holding back. It's time you let it out . . . and I think it would help your case a lot, too."

"Leyla, what are you talking about? I don't have any explosive material in my office."

"Don't underestimate me, Jack," she said. "Let me see the photo of that slippery little mule."

Londoño looked at her as if he had a question mark tattooed across his forehead.

"Photo? What photo? I don't know what you're talking about. I'd love to have a photo of the people I'm investigating. But I haven't got anything, Leyla, so please, I have to ask you to leave."

"All right, Detective, I understand. You don't have the time. But what do you say we get together a little later— we can have a cup of coffee, and who knows? Between the two of us, maybe we can crack the case of this mysterious mule. I finish the news at six-thirty and I could meet you, say, about an hour later, seven-thirty? What do you say?"

"Today, Tuesday, you mean?" he asked, with a touch of impatience.

"Yes, why not?"

"Not possible, Leyla. You'll have to forgive me but I'm busy tonight. I'm sorry, but tonight is out of the question."

He almost had to physically push her out of his office. The truth is, Jack Londoño couldn't stand Leyla Sonora—even the perfume she wore was annoying. He glanced down at his watch: it was two in the afternoon, eight hours until he would get to see Tania. In the meantime, he had to get to work. And as he got to thinking, Leyla's comment, though annoying, did pique his curiosity. What photo was she talking about?

He went to ask Gil, but he wasn't in his office, as usual, so he decided to phone Fernando Padrón. Was it possible he knew something? It had been several days since they had last spoken at Fernando Travel. He dialed the number and the phone rang and rang, but nobody picked up, so he dropped the idea for the moment, grabbed his jacket, and walked down the stairs to get his car and head out to

Rikers Island. He had a number of people to interrogate that afternoon.

Whenever Leyla Sonora appeared on Northern Boulevard, her arrival was always heralded by the clicking of her high heels, like an orchestra of perfectly synchronized drummers, the rhythms of which reverberated up and down the avenue. Today was no exception. With a pair of bright red pumps on her feet and a matching purse slung over her shoulder, she strutted down the street, her voluptuous body squeezed into a clingy sand-colored suit. Saluting the passersby like a candidate at the height of campaign season, or a carnival queen waving to her subjects from a float, she smiled at one and all, called out to some people by name, and planted juicy kisses on the cheeks of a lucky few. She walked into restaurants and newsstands to chirp good morning, she stopped to chat with the lady who sold the magic essences and medicinal herbs, but her most affectionate greeting of all was reserved for the sidewalk vendors of arepas, tamales, and enchiladas.

Leyla loved walking down those streets. The hustle and bustle reminded her of her childhood in Havana, of the days when she would hold tight on to her mother's hand as they went shopping in the city streets. Or those Sunday mornings when her grandfather would take her with him to the Mercado Único in Havana. She loved flirting with all the friends she'd made in this working-class New York neighborhood; she felt appreciated and welcomed in this Latin-American environment, and that feeling wasn't so easy to come by in the United States.

"Save me a little *sancocho, mi gordo bello,*" Leyla cooed to

Jeremías in her velvety voice, so perfectly calibrated for seduction. Jeremías was a good-natured Colombian who fed all the needy souls who approached the door to his tiny luncheonette. In his house, as a little boy, his mother and grandmother had always done the same, serving up food to people who had fallen upon rough times. His grandmother believed that to share a plate of food was a blessing.

Countless times Leyla had whiled away the hours with Jeremías, savoring his delicious beef stew. She knew what a good man he was, a man for whom the act of cooking was the purest form of happiness. Aside from the fact that she truly adored stopping by his luncheonette, tasting the stews and chatting with Jeremías, she also lingered there because she knew that between spoonfuls of *sancocho*, people had a tendency to confess their deepest secrets to Jeremías, an engaging conversationalist whose strong suit was not silence. On more than one occasion, Leyla had gotten information from him that had helped uncover the truth about some or other story in Little Colombia.

After her very Caribbean stroll through the neighborhood, Leyla went over to Fernando Travel. As she opened the door, she had to inch her way past the many people milling around in the smallest but busiest storefront on Roosevelt Avenue. Towering and magnificent, Leyla advanced implacably toward Fernando's desk as if she were preparing to reveal a terrible secret. When the people saw her coming they all stepped aside, as if making way for a Virgin in a procession. Sitting behind his desk, Fernando smiled, and thanked the retreating crowds for letting Leyla Sonora past them.

"Hello, my sexy *gordo*," she called out, like a playful femme fatale, revealing the affection and admiration she felt for Fernando. "Listen, I have some names here that I'm hoping you can confirm. Yesterday I got together with Londoño, and you know, I know they say that nothing gets past him, that he's such a bloodhound, but . . . that man really confuses me sometimes . . ."

"Why, Leyla?" Fernando adored it when Leyla digressed like this. She would never, of course, lose sight of her real reason for visiting him, but these sidebar discussions had a way of making their conversations so much more entertaining.

"Because sometimes I swear he seems more Scandinavian than Puerto Rican," she said, taking a deep breath. "But anyway, he confirmed what I knew about the girl—you know, the mule everyone is looking for but can't seem to find."

"Londoño confirmed something about an imaginary mule?" Fernando asked, trying to skirt the topic a bit.

"Don't play dumb with me, Ferni, this mule is anything but imaginary. It seems that this girl has outsmarted the smartest of those cops . . ."

"Is that what Londoño told you? How modest of him."

"Come on now, don't try to slip out of this one . . ."

"Well, I just find that hard to believe . . ."

"Hmm. You know me too well. All right, the Puerto Rican Swede did not confirm it for me, but he didn't deny it either. Let's just say he remained silent . . . and while maybe it wasn't exactly a conspiratorial kind of silence, it was pretty suspicious."

Fernando sighed with relief.

"Leyla, calm down and quit theorizing. You haven't confirmed anything yet."

"Come on, Fernando. You know as well as I do that journalism is all about coming up with theories and proving them with whatever leads you've got. So no, I haven't confirmed it, my darling Fernando, and that is why I have come to see you. I just need a couple of details. According to what they tell me out there on the street, the little mule everyone's looking for is the girlfriend of a big-time drug dealer *and* a cop. She's a very young, very sharp girl, this Colombian . . ."

"Leyla, I'm telling you, you can't just go around speculating like that," Fernando said, exasperated. She eyed him suspiciously.

"You know what, my friend? I believe that you have this entire story documented. You must have letters and photos in your archives, I know it. Don't tell me you haven't heard from the girl's parents, some kind of letter from her family asking you to look for her. . . . Come on, Ferni, don't be selfish, share your information with me. We're on the same side, and it's my one missing link. From what I hear, this girl has smuggled drugs into the country as if they were coffee beans, paid no taxes, nothing. Don't go telling me that the only thing anyone knows about her is that airport video . . ."

"Nothing gets past you, does it, sweetheart?" Fernando sighed.

"Listen, Ferni, I know you have something. Look, here's my list with all the names, all the flights, all the mules. This girl is key because in addition to sleeping with her, that drug dealer uses her to interface with his big-time contacts. And on top of everything, rumor has it that she's gone underground now, trying to get classified information for her boss. That's everything I know, and I'm telling it to you straight, so now it's your turn. Come on, it's only fair . . ."

Fernando knew that she wouldn't stop until she got all the information she was after. She sniffed out the information, focused all her energies on confirming her leads, and she would hound him all day if she had to, to get what she wanted in the end.

"Listen, we're not sure, but a few days ago we got a letter from Medellín, from a mother asking me to look for her daughter . . ."

Leyla laughed and clapped her hands three times over her head in triumph.

"Bingo! Show me the letter."

"I can't, Leyla. I handed it over to Gil, the detective, the one that works with Londoño."

"Did the letter come with a photo?"

"Yes."

"And you handed over both? I don't believe it! You can't be serious! You never do that, Fernando!"

She tried every argument she could think of, and even a few she dreamed up on the spot, turning the issue upside down and inside out, reminding Fernando of the thousands of times she'd helped him out on other occasions, but it was all useless. Fernando wasn't talking. But in the end, exhausted by the verbal sparring that she thought she had lost, Leyla Sonora finally got the information she needed to connect the final dot in her investigation.

Sweating profusely, as if he'd just run an obstacle course, Fernando finally gave in:

"Her name is Lucila Santa María, but they call her Lucy."

Only then did Leyla stand up to leave, savoring the triumph and preparing herself to go after the last few things she needed to put together her news report.

As soon as Leyla left, Fernando started digging through the second drawer in his desk until he located a manila folder with a metal clasp. Inside were several letters in their original envelopes, and he flipped through them until he found the one he was looking for: a blue envelope with his name and address written in large, firm script. Opening the envelope flap, he removed a letter signed by Doña Antonia Arbilla, a letter filled with anguish, written by a mother in agony.

Dear Don Fernando:

I am taking the liberty of writing to you because I know that you are the only person who can help me. My name is Antonia Arbilla, and I am the mother of Lucila Santa María, a 23-year-old girl who looks much younger than she really is; at first glance people often think she is underage. I am enclosing a photograph to give you an idea of what she looks like. She is my only daughter, and a year ago she traveled to the United States to work as a maid in the home of the Rentarías, a Colombian family. Ever since then, my Lucy has called me every week without fail until three months ago, when the phone calls suddenly stopped. She had given me a telephone number, 974-555-7264 to locate her in case of a family emergency, and I have tried calling this number many times to no avail.

My daughter is a fragile-looking girl but in reality she is a very determined young woman, she has always been that way. She is thin, and has a beauty mark on her left shoulder and blond hair which was shoulder length when she left home last year.

Don Fernando, I know you are a busy man and that many people come to you asking for favors. And I also know that what I am asking for is a miracle. I am asking you to help me find the one person in the world who is more important to me than life itself, because I have lost her. In exchange, you may ask whatever you wish of me, and I will give it to you. All I want is to see my daughter again, to know that she is alive, no matter where she is, walking freely down the street or in prison for her mistakes.

Please, Don Fernando, please tell me that Lucy is still in this world. Please tell me that I will see her beautiful golden eyes again, the same eyes that looked up at me when she was a little girl. Please tell me that I will be able to stroke her soft hair, as bright and lovely as the light of the angels. Tell me, Don Fernando, that my daughter still sees the light of day and breathes in the cold night air. Whatever happened, whatever she may have done or not done, none of that matters to me.

I will pay for her mistakes with my life if I must. I will wipe away her mistakes with the same blood that gave her life. But please, tell me that my Lucy is still out there somewhere, please tell me that one day, I don't care where or when, that I will once again be able to hold her in my arms, my daughter, the only daughter that God gave me. Please tell me that I will one day be able to hear her heart beating, her voice calling out to me and her footsteps as she walks toward me.

Don Fernando, I know what it is like to live with death, because that is how I have felt ever since the day she left. She told me it would only be for a little while, that she was going to go to work in the United States for a family that would take care of her papers, and that she would save up her money and come home so that we could open a little business together.

Please, Don Fernando, help me find her. It has been three months since I last heard from her. For three months I haven't received a single phone call, letter, or message. I hope that this letter will remain in your hands only, Don Fernando. And I hope you keep it in your heart, too.

With all my hope,
Antonia Arbilla

This was not the first letter of this type, nor would it be the last, to pass through his hands. This time, however, like never before, Fernando felt the full weight of the responsibility that he had assumed. He knew that these people wrote to him because he was their last hope. He dried his tears and sat there for a little while, staring off into the distance.

The streets of Little Colombia were teeming with people. How many of those young men crossing the street would disappear one day? How many of them would die from bullets fired by the mafia? How many of them would end up with an exploded capsule of cocaine in their bellies?

He folded up Antonia's letter and carefully wrote down the number that Lucy had given her: 974-555-7264. Following the procedure he knew by heart, he opened one of the drawers in his big closet and removed the notebook where he kept information on the mafiosos in Jackson Heights. It was a list of names, phone numbers, and addresses that Londoño had once given him when he needed to corroborate some information. Gritting his teeth, he prayed that Lucy's number wouldn't match any of the ones on his list, but there it was, the exact same number that appeared last on Londoño's list. It was the telephone number of Darío Rengifo, second-in-command to Braulio Rentaría, the man who moved massive drug shipments from his headquarters in Flushing, Queens, and who had a hand-picked team of the best and brightest mules in the business. He never missed. He ran circles around the police.

So that was where Lucy had ended up. Lucy, Antonia Arbilla's little angel.

This wasn't the moment for tears, however. Fernando reviewed Lucy's picture again: straight light brown hair; honey-colored eyes, and a small snub nose. She did seem to fit the description of the mysterious mule the police were looking for, and so he picked up the phone to call Londoño's office, but he wasn't there. Guillermo Gil, his assistant, picked up the line, and as soon as he heard the urgency in Fernando's voice he said he'd be right over. In no time at all Gil was sitting in Fernando's office.

"I already gave him a folder that I prepared with files on all the most important mules, but I'm sure that when he sees this—"

"Be very careful with this information, son," Fernando warned. "You know as well as I do that the mafia has ears on the walls and eyes in the electrical outlets. Leave me a copy of the letter and take the photo with you."

"Damn!" said Gil as he looked down at the snapshot. "She's something else . . . Her poor mother. What would she say if she knew she'd never lay eyes on her daughter again . . ."

"Shut your mouth, man! Let's not bury her yet."

Fernando stood up from his chair and went outside to take a few deep breaths. Antonia Arbilla's letter had saddened him. As he walked through his neighborhood, images of all the people who had left him passed before his eyes. The last person whom he thought of was Adrián . . . where was he? Would Lucy end up like one of them? He clenched his teeth and felt the wind whip across his face. He needed to keep his emotions in check. But more than anything, he needed to know what it felt like to rescue another victim from the jaws of death. He filled his lungs with air, and concentrated on doing the right thing.

Lucy had been feeling nauseous ever since the early dawn hours: her mouth was bitter, her head was pounding, and all she wanted to do was crawl under the covers and go to sleep for a week. This was a turn of events that she hadn't prepared for. She didn't know for sure, but she suspected that she might be pregnant with Jack's baby.

What would Braulio say if he ever found out? How would he kill her? With one shot? No, that would be too kind. Throughout everything, she had managed to control her emotions, somehow she had managed to keep things from getting out of hand. She loved the policeman with every bone in her body, but she had covered her tracks pretty well, by feeding Braulio stories about Darío Rengifo's betrayal. It was pure fiction and it had infuriated Braulio, but it was what had allowed her to continue seeing Londoño indefinitely. But that wasn't all she'd done: she had also kept herself busy hunting through the house where Braulio kept her locked away. She knew all the bedrooms, all the secret exits, and, most important, she had discovered where they hid the bags of drugs brought into the country by mules.

How many of those little bags would she need to buy her freedom? She didn't have time to think. It was two in the afternoon: snack time. Tiptoeing out the door of her room, she headed down the hallway in the direction of her objective. At that hour, everyone was gone. With her heart pounding like a hammer in her chest, she turned the key in the lock and quickly entered the room. She was wearing a pair of roomy overalls with a massive inner pocket, right at stomach level, made of a bedsheet that she had ripped up and sewn on.

Her hands trembling, she opened the closet where they kept the capsules before processing them, and she filled her pocket with as many as she could, picking up the ones that fell to the floor, careful not to leave a trail behind her. Then she left, as fast as she could, grabbing a blue cape that covered her down to her knees, and hurried toward the far end of the yard. Undetected, she walked through the gate and crossed the massive lawn that separated the house from the outside world. That was when she broke into a run, like a soul in agony. With her heart throbbing in her temples, she ran and ran and ran and she didn't stop. "God help me, God help me," she repeated to herself over and over again.

When she finally reached Queens Boulevard, she jumped onto the first bus that passed by and stayed on for the entire route, getting off at the last stop. There, she took another bus and sat out the ride until it was finally time to call Lola. Lola had promised her that in exchange for a few bags of cocaine, she would give Lucy new documents that would get her out of the country.

Would Lola be her salvation?

Just as he did every Tuesday, Jack entered the Chibcha at 9:30 P.M. for his weekly date with the woman of his life. When he walked in and didn't see her sitting in her usual spot, he felt a skittish, empty feeling that made him shiver. He scanned the bar, but she was nowhere to be found. He waited one hour, then another, but Tania didn't turn up, nor did she call his cell phone. He had made her memorize his number in case she needed to get through to him in an emergency. Something awful had happened to her; he knew it. Something awful, but he didn't know what.

He walked over to the bar and asked the bartender on shift if he had seen her come in earlier and leave with someone else, or if she had left him a message. The bartender just shook his head. Londoño could feel the smell of misfortune enveloping him, inevitable and implacable, closing in on him. Finally he left the bar and began combing the streets of Jackson Heights like a madman, like a wounded bloodhound in search of his prey. Nothing. No sign at all of the woman he had thought was his.

But who was she, really? Who was Tania Castellanos and why hadn't he ever wondered before? Like so many times before, his desperation and anguish led him to his office at the police station. Climbing the stairs two at a time, he asked the guard on duty if there had been any accidents reported in the area.

"Quiet night, boss," he responded. Londoño headed for his office. His hands were ice-cold.

At eight P.M. Lucy and Lola met. Lucy was shaking like a leaf, and the older woman cautiously averted her gaze.

"My hands are frozen, Lola," said Lucy when they found each other on the stairway of the Queens Boulevard train station. Lola went pale, and avoided looking her in the eye. Together they walked over to a nearby building, took the elevator up, and entered a simple but immaculate apartment. Without even taking off her coat, the woman, much more aloof than usual, said,

"Wait here a little while. I'll be back in just a few minutes."

She left the apartment, closing the door behind her. The minute she was gone, Tania could tell that something was amiss. As if catapulted by a spring, she jumped to her feet, dizzy. Closing her eyes, she took several deep breaths until she recovered her balance. Then she got moving: first she went into the bathroom and closed the lock from the inside, making sure the door was fully shut. Then she opened the window that led to the fire escape, raised it high, and stepped outside. Before descending the stairs, she lowered the window back to its original position and raced down the fire escape. When she made it to the street level, she clung tight to the side of the building, breathed deeply, and pushed the ladder back up into place so that it would look as though it hadn't been used.

Crouching down low, she ran down the alley behind the building. Suddenly she remembered that she had a hat in her bag, pulled it out, and put it on. With her head covered, she removed her cape and put it back on inside out, with the gray lining on the outside. Somewhat transformed, she ran toward the Queens Boulevard subway station but then thought better of it: that was the first place they'd go looking for her. Instead, she hailed a cab and called Jack on his cell phone.

Londoño was desperate, his mind racing round and round in circles. He didn't know what to do. Where could she be? Who could tell him where she was? His desk was strewn with papers, filled with information on mules who were either dead or had never resurfaced. Gil had prepared the latest file, but the girl they were looking for wasn't there. The day before, however, his assistant had tried to talk to him about number 10. Surveying his desk, his eyes stopped on the manila folder with the number 9 crossed out and a number 10 underneath. He opened it. Finally, he held in his hands a photograph of the mule they all wanted to get their hands on! But his surprise quickly gave way to shock when he recognized the face in the photo. It was Tania. Yes, it was Tania, all right, but with longer, light brown hair. There was no doubt about it, those were her eyes, her face . . . Londoño felt a tremor run through his body, and pressed the photograph against his chest.

Right then his cell phone rang. The caller ID showed an unknown number. He hesitated for a second before picking up.

"Jack, is that you?"

"Tania?"

"Jack, my life is in danger, I need you . . . I'll explain everything when I see you."

"Where are you?"

"On Queens Boulevard, I just got into a taxi. They're already after me, I know it . . ."

"Tell the driver to take you to the Jackson Heights station, get out, and look for me. I'll be waiting for you."

"Jack . . . ?"

"Yes . . . ?"

"Can you ever forgive me for lying to you?"

"This isn't the time. . . . Right now we have to get you somewhere safe before Rentaría finds you. That's what's important."

"Jack, how did you know?"

"This isn't the time for explanations, Tania . . ."

"Jack?"

"Yes?"

"I love you . . ."

"I love you, too. Now, let's meet at the entrance to the Jackson Heights station."

As he drove over to the Jackson Heights subway station, Londoño dialed Fernando Padrón's private number. It rang several times before Fernando picked up.

"Hello?" he said, half asleep.

"Don Fernando, it's me, Jack Londoño. I need your help, it's a life-or-death situation for Lucy . . ."

"I'll do whatever I can," he responded firmly. "What's happened?"

"All I ask is that you open the door to your building when I buzz you."

"Fine. How long will you be?"

"Within the next twenty minutes we should be there."

"Both of you?"

"That's right."

"Thank God! We have to get her out of here as fast as we can. I'm going to make a few phone calls."

"In complete confidence, I have to tell you: they're looking for her."

"I bet they are."

They hung up in unison. Fernando then dialed a couple of old friends, his most trusted collaborators. He was beginning to enjoy this, because he had a feeling that they would save Lucy's life. He had a feeling that a miracle was about to take place, one that would foil the odds stacked against her.

Both of the friends he telephoned promised they would be at Fernando's house in thirty minutes.

In the two hours that followed, Coco Sattui put his talents as a stylist to work, creating both makeup and wardrobe to disguise Lucy and Jack. They would be playing the roles of their lives as they traveled to the destiny that awaited them. As Coco worked on Lucy, Jack made reservations for a flight that would take them from Newark to Chicago and then directly to San Juan, Puerto Rico, where he had friends who would take them to a secret location. A place where he and Lucy would start a new life together. Fernando would take care of communicating with Doña Antonia.

The days that followed were utter chaos. Fernando was the contact through whom Gil discovered the safe houses of Braulio Rentaría, and as perfectly as if they had found a map to guide their way, federal agents went straight to the room where the mafioso kept the bags of cocaine that Braulio's mules had swallowed and delivered to him. It was plenty: more than enough to lock him away for a very long time.

Leyla Sonora scored yet another journalistic coup when she and her team arrived at Rentaría's house and taped the federal agents leaving with all the contraband Rentaría had stockpiled there. Thanks to this scoop, Leyla confirmed her status as one of the most respected and well-loved media personalities among the Latin-American community in New York. She had become a veritable authority on mules and drug trafficking.

One afternoon, after answering an endless round of questions from other journalists who were clamoring to talk to her, Leyla sought refuge in Fernando Travel.

"Oh, *mi gordo,* what do you say we go out to dinner in a little while?"

"That sounds marvelous, darling. Eight on the dot at Pollos Mario?"

"Perfect, *mi gordo bello.* I'll look for you there

then . . . but, well, why don't we just go now? It's already seven-thirty . . ."

"Yes, why not? You're always on the ball, you know that?"

Everyone turned around to catch a glimpse of them.

"I can't believe it, *mi gordo bello*, we have turned into real-life celebrities!"

"You're the only celebrity here, darling, I'm just a poor, simple neighborhood accountant."

"Don't you play modest with me. You know you are the best, most marvelous, most adored *gordo* in all of New York."

"And you the most flattering journalist."

"So, tell me . . . what do you know about our disappeared friend?"

"Who are you talking about?"

"You know exactly who I'm talking about."

"I swear to you I don't."

"If I were to ask you about an old friend who, according to rumor, maintained a relationship with a girl who all of us were looking for but nobody ever officially found, what would you say to me?"

"That there're a lot of old friends who suddenly disappear, people who we look for but never find, but we just keep on hoping and praying that wherever they are, their lives are happy ones."

"Oh, *gordito*, one of these days I'm going to declare my love for you!"

"Let's keep our relationship within the bounds of propriety, what do you say?"

"Well, if you insist."

"I do . . ."

It was just before ten P.M. and Fernando was getting ready to ask for the check when he looked out the window and noticed a young man step away from his motorcycle. It was instinct more than anything: challenging his bulky physique, Fernando suddenly lunged forward onto Leyla, pinning her to the floor just as a shot rang out in the restaurant, and a bullet shattered the window facing the street.

The next morning, the attempted murder of Leyla Sonora made the front page of newspapers all over the world. And Fernando's act of courage earned him a commemorative medal that New York mayor Michael Bloomberg handed to him, describing him as a guardian angel looking out over the city of New York. A living angel in Jackson Heights.

11

A New Beginning

Restless in his bed, his eyes blinked rapidly, incessantly.

"*Ave María, Madre!*" Fernando cried out. Rubbing his eyes, he got up from the bed as if someone had pushed him, and stumbled around his bedroom before getting his bearings. Sitting down in a chair, he tried to calm himself down, so that he could think straight and make sense of the nightmare he'd just had.

In his dreams he had seen a woman, motionless, lying upon a rough wooden table, surrounded by candles and women reciting the rosary. As he moved closer, he was dumbfounded by what he saw: the person they were all praying for was his mother. Without even waking up, he began to mutter,

"My mother, it's my mother."

He went over to the telephone and dialed the number of his mother, Doña Lucrecia Mendoza. It rang several times before the answering machine finally picked up, with a new message:

"Blessings, leave your message or call back after next Sunday." That was when he remembered what she had told him the last time he had seen her: she was going to Colombia, "just for a few days, to bring Claudia some clothes, now that she's about to have her baby." Claudia was Doña Lucrecia's niece; Doña Lucrecia had raised Claudia herself, in her own home, and she loved the girl dearly. Fernando called the Avianca check-in counter, but for some reason nobody picked up.

Doña Lucrecia Mendoza had already embarked, as she often did, on the Bogotá flight that left in the early dawn hours. She traveled frequently to Colombia, bringing clothes, provisions, and hope to the many charitable organizations she worked with from New York. She always insisted on going to the airport alone, saying it was pointless to wake up her children to ask them to take her to the airport. She was fierce about maintaining her independence, and since she flew so frequently (having taken her very first flight twenty-five years earlier), she never bothered to call her children to say good-bye, more than anything so that they wouldn't insist on taking her to the airport. As she always said to them, "Everyone has to work—why should you lose a good night's sleep on account of me?"

At seventy-five years of age, Doña Lucrecia Mendoza

was in fine form. Aside from a slight rise in her blood pressure and weight, she was in terrific shape thanks to the physical activity to which she had been accustomed ever since she was a young girl helping her parents in the fields. Years later when her husband, an accountant, left her for his secretary, she wasted no time crying over her predicament, nor did she blame the world, or rail against God for putting her through such a harrowing experience.

Instead, she went out and bought enough flour to make a mountain of her delicious empanadas, and then she bought a pretty basket which she decorated with ribbons and flowers from her garden. With the basket perched upon her head, she went out onto the street and sold out her empanadas in no time at all. Soon she began taking special orders and ended up making a business out of it, a business that allowed her to stay at home and take care of her children while the fruits of her labor earned them the money they needed to get by. She also cleaned out the rooms that her husband had previously used as a waiting room and office and turned them into bedrooms that she rented out to students from the provinces who came to study in the city.

"There's no point in crying over these things. Problems get solved with firm action," she loved to say to her children. And she practiced what she preached, taking firm actions when she had to, facing each setback with her customary fighting spirit. She worked hard to raise her kids, and she did it with a tenacity and an optimism that she cultivated throughout her entire life. She believed that these were essential qualities for doing good, which is what she always did.

That was the reason she shared such a special bond with her oldest son, Fernandito, who was also her favorite, probably because he seemed to have inherited that spirit of hers. And that was what made her come to New York when he urged her to move there. At first she had a difficult time comprehending the seeming indifference of all those people who just walked past beggars as if nothing at all was wrong. But little by little, as a reaction to this, she decided that her job in the United States would be to help as many needy people as she could. She wanted to bring a bit of optimism and good cheer to her compatriots.

She had always been especially sensitive to the hunger and the scarcity that was so prevalent among her countrymen, and before she knew it, her mailbox was literally overflowing with letters from old neighbors, friends, and even the parish priest from her church in Medellín. There were so many in need back in Colombia, and here she was, enjoying such abundance. This, then, was what drove her, time and again, to board a plane for Colombia, always with hefty overweight fees for her luggage. Everyone at the Avianca check-in counter knew her; new employees always whispered about her, hypothesizing that she was going home to open a store, or some kind of business. In fact she did open something—not a store but a center to help people who didn't have money to buy things like clothes and shoes, a place where they could get things like soap, shampoo, deodorant, canned goods, first-aid medicine, and other basic items.

It didn't take her long to figure out how to request aid from New York's charitable institutions. Little by little she earned the trust, respect, and affection of the leaders of many of these groups, and they helped her obtain all sorts of assistance. Often people left massive boxes filled with donations in the office of her son Fernandito, and later she would busy herself sorting and packing everything with the diligence of a missionary. Months before the Christmas season, she would request and receive packages with gifts that she would separate by category—age, style, size—and then lovingly wrap up in festive paper, imagining the faces of those little angels as they opened their presents on Christmas Eve after Santa Claus's official visit.

"Mother, don't you ever get tired of working?"

"Listen, I have been blessed with good health and much more than I need in life. I have all the luxuries that you have found a way to give me. I don't have to work; you don't even let me clean the house you bought me. The least I can do is take an interest in those people who have nothing at all."

"You don't know how much I admire you, Mother."

"I say the same to you, my son, I say the same to you."

Then they hugged, grateful that they had each other.

Fernando's mother also had a very well-honed sixth sense, and paid a good deal of attention to dreams, premonitions, and nightmares, which she interpreted as coded information, and warnings that arrived from another realm. She also listened to the predictions of clairvoyants and to the wisdom gleaned from tarot card readings. She still remembered, very clearly, an adolescent visit to an old witch doctor who predicted that she would have four children whom she would raise on her own, and that one day one of her children would take her, through the air, to a huge, faraway city with many, many people. That was one of her favorite anecdotes, and she loved to repeat it in the company of people who were skeptical of such prophecies.

Just as the psychic predicted, as soon as Fernando brought his siblings over to New York, he began trying to bring his good mother over, too, for he missed her more and more with each passing day.

Having been promoted to assistant manager of one of Don Pietro Colombo's restaurants in Manhattan, Fernando supported his younger siblings until they got on their feet, and then he saved up enough money to buy his mother a house. By that time, he was already in negotiations to open his own office. Don Pietro approved of his plans, and supported him on both fronts, getting him an excellent price for the house Fernando bought in Jackson Heights, close to the newly acquired storefront where he would soon hang out his shingle as an accountant and travel agent.

Doña Lucrecia was stunned when she laid eyes on the house her son had bought her.

"Fernandito, my son! I can't imagine how hard you must have worked to get the money for this house . . ."

"Do you like it, Mother?"

"Of course I do, son. It is a beautiful home."

"It's a little small, don't you think, Mother?" That was his sister, Patricia.

"No, dear, no—it's exactly what I need."

"Why did you say thank you only to Fernando? Don't you think we're capable of buying you a house, too?"

"I believe you are capable of doing whatever you set your mind to, but I know you well, and I know that Fernando was the one who bought this house. Or am I wrong?"

"Well, I told him he didn't have to buy you a house, that he should have just rented you an apartment and given us, his brothers and me, his sister, the money to start a business, so that we wouldn't have to answer to some boss anymore. But he's so selfish, he told me that if I wanted my own business I had to work for it. He just said that he saved that money to buy a house. He's so selfish!"

"Oh, really?"

There had always been a deep sense of rivalry among Lucrecia's children, who were all keenly aware of the great love their mother lavished upon her oldest son. They never stopped to consider, though, that perhaps Fernando's behavior was the reason that their mother had such faith and trust in him and not them. In addition, all the things Fernando did on behalf of the needy were a direct result of the example his mother had set for him. This united Doña Lucrecia and her son even more, but it also created a rift between Fernando and his siblings, a rift that grew deeper all the time.

The next few minutes were exasperating and desperate ones, as Fernando kept dialing Avianca's number, to no avail. That was when he turned on the television and heard the most traumatic news of his life. Fernando felt a sharp pain pierce him in the center of his chest as he heard that the Avianca Airlines Boeing 727-321 had disappeared into the ocean with over seventy passengers on board. He watched, numb, as the television cameras panned across the inscrutable surface of the Atlantic.

No bodies had been found, but Fernando felt certain that his mother had managed to escape, that she had put on her life jacket in time. He was convinced that after helping out her neighbor Doña Lucrecia had saved her own life by virtue of her steadfast temperament.

The days went by, and finally, when there was no longer any possibility that she could have survived, Fernando drew his brother and sister toward him in a tight embrace, feeling deeply vulnerable. It was as if a protective bubble around him had popped, leaving him exposed to the harsh elements of the world. He could not conceive of life without the presence of his mother. She had always been there for him, at every single moment of his life. Firm and decisive, she had always challenged her children to improve, to overcome obstacles, and to do the very best they could at all times.

He thought back to the day he started working at his uncle's bottling plant, and the day he collected his first paycheck. As he handed it over to his mother, Doña Lucrecia said to him:

"Fernando, a new life begins today for you: from now on, nothing can stop you." She supported him wholeheartedly when he decided to go to the United States, and during his first few months as a restaurant dishwasher. She always reminded him that all beginnings were hard, but that after a while he would be proud of having achieved his goals all on his own, without any tricks or subterfuge. Over and over again, she would tell him that the important thing was to be able to sleep at night and look himself in the mirror without being scared of his reflection.

And that was what he had done. He had overcome the

obstacles, just as she had overcome her fear of flying. That, actually, was part of why she downplayed the whole process of going to the airport, so that she wouldn't feel worse before leaving. The important thing, she always said, was achieving the goal, the objective, of helping other people. "My fear is the result of nonsense," she would always say, smiling.

He missed her even more now than he had when he had first arrived in New York, because in the old days he had no memories of her in the city. Now all the corners and streets they had explored together reminded him painfully of the things she had said, and of her wise instincts regarding people and places.

Only after all of her children were safely settled in New York had she agreed to make the move herself. Fernando went to Colombia to pick her up, holding her hand as they said good-bye to the city where she was born, where her children were born, and where she raised her family. Doña Lucrecia surprised Fernando that day by bringing him to a shack in one of Medellín's more marginal neighborhoods. It was a desperately poor place where the houses had no windows, no electricity; it was another world for him. In front of the shack, a large group of people had gathered and were waiting patiently. Fernando and his mother joined them and after a short while, for the first time in his life, Fernando found himself in the presence of a *curandero*, a witch doctor, who predicted a promising future for them: "You will travel a great deal, my daughter," he told Lucrecia as he gazed off into the distance. "Prepare yourself for a surprising ride." Fernando, oddly perturbed by all of this, jumped up and left the shack, frightened.

His friends in the fire and police departments allowed him to join them on their search-and-rescue missions, but there was little or nothing to rescue. All they could do was explore the vast expanses of open sea where they found nothing other than dark, silent water. "My God, where is my mother?" Fernando asked himself day and night, everywhere he went. The following months were long and hard, not knowing where she was, or what to do with the unspeakable pain he felt. Dr. Murtúa promised Fernando that the minute he heard anything he would contact him immediately, but Fernando regularly visited the morgue on his own, just to check up on things himself.

After two weeks the authorities concluded that whatever they hadn't been able to find so far, couldn't be found. The search-and-rescue missions came to an end. Knowing so certainly, so definitively, that he would never find his mother's remains, that he would never be able to say goodbye to her, consumed Fernando with the greatest heartache he had ever known. Priests and rabbis he knew stopped by to help him through this difficult period, but Fernando was unable to make any sense of the senseless nature of death.

Thanks to the black box that was found during the search-and-rescue missions, the authorities were able to reconstruct the minutes leading up to the accident, and discovered that there had been a mechanical problem: a mechanical problem that had been overlooked that could have been fixed before takeoff. The captain had tried to return to the airport, but given the situation, he had been forced to attempt an emergency landing on an airstrip that could sustain the impact. It seemed that he tried, but the old equipment did not respond as it should have. Because of the impact, it was believed that the passengers suffered an instant, almost painless death. None of this, however, was of any comfort to the family members gripped by the grief and anguish over the death of their loved ones.

An immense void took root inside of Fernando and stayed with him for a long, long time. He tried to get closer to his brothers and sister, to create a tighter family nucleus, a cycle of blood and pain, of shared experiences and mutual protection. A nucleus that could shield them from the blows that life might deliver. In the aftermath of their loss, he tried to achieve what he thought his good mother would have wanted for her children: a more united family whose members protected and looked after one another just as she had when she was alive.

That, however, was not the path that life had in store for him.

In general, excessive ambition never makes very good company. Fernando's sister, Patricia, was the first person to mention the topic of a lawsuit that might bring them some kind of compensation. Tall and decisive, she had intense eyes and a relentless determination to achieve the American Dream. She had adapted to the demands of life in the United States with little trouble, and married a noble, hard-working American whom she ordered around as she pleased. Together, they had had three children whom Fernando adored. He would smile from ear to ear as he taught them mathematics and coordination games, and every time their mother punished them for silly things, they would seek out their Uncle Fern. This, of course, often meant that mother and uncle would have it out in heated discussions that always ended with Patricia slamming the door and with children emerging victorious.

While Patricia certainly inherited her mother's swiftness, she also possessed a formidable instinct for greed, something that was completely anathema to Doña Lucrecia. Patricia's unbridled desire for wealth was a driving force that consumed her entire existence. Nothing was enough for her; she was impossible to satisfy, stubborn and self-centered. The slightest obstacle turned her world upside down. When her mother died, however, she recovered without shedding a tear, except when she was in a legal environment—on those occasions, she dramatized her experience to such a degree that, several times, the lawyers for the airline looked absolutely distraught.

Fernando was flabbergasted as he observed the histrionic talents of the woman who had once been his little sister. There was nothing little about her anymore, that was for sure. And he was stunned by the fact that she could so easily ascribe a monetary value to pain, to something so very irreparable, as if it were a rug that had been damaged, or a smashed-up car that could simply be replaced by another.

Though he disagreed with the idea from the outset, Fernando headed up their side of the lawsuit, which he knew would be a long-drawn-out process that might very well go on for months or even years. It was a situation that debilitated all the people involved, who, every so often, would be forced to dredge up the memory of those grim days and live through them all over again.

As all this was happening, Fernando found himself unable to do anything to prevent the disintegration of the family that Doña Lucrecia, with such love and such sacrifice, had created out of nothing. When she left, everything fell to pieces. The tiniest little things set off such bitter arguments between him and the brothers who still lived in the house that one fine day they packed their things and left.

Fernando, so adept at solving other people's crises, failed to realize that the one thing holding his family together was the fabric his mother had so carefully woven. When she died, the threads simply unraveled, and Fernando was left not only with a tremendous feeling of solitude but with the sensation that he had failed somehow, that he had been the reason his family had fallen apart. Only Patricia, with whom Fernando had serious differences, continued living in her mother's home, and he was so focused on keeping the family intact that he failed to see what was really going on.

The arguments went on and on: they fought over anything and everything. The least little thing was liable to set Patricia off because, in essence, she couldn't stand her brother's lifestyle, his generosity, his unflappable austerity, the disarray in which he functioned so effortlessly. Patricia, who worked in the field of insurance sales, despised Fernando's world, most especially the atmosphere that for her was just "too Colombian." She was also bothered by Fernando's commitment to his fellow man, by his ability to summarily drop his money-making activities in order to help a bunch of strangers with problems. With her silent husband, she complained bitterly of "my stupid brother, always with that line of poor slobs that he treats like nobility." Patricia's husband observed her without flinching.

Sometimes she told Fernando off to his face:

"Why do you bring those people into the agency? All they do is drive away business, real clients, not people like them—all they want is favors from you. You're such a stupid shit . . ."

Patricia dreamed of an existence far removed from the Latin-American world in which she lived. And she was willing to work as hard as she had to if, in the end, it would help provide her an escape. For her, work was a necessary evil for achieving certain goals: prosperity, glamour, luxuries. In the middle of all these aspirations, her brother was too strong a contrast. She simply couldn't tolerate her brother, and all the stupid things he was always doing, writing in his diaries, jotting down all those stories.

She often made fun of him, and sometimes her mocking attitude led to nasty disputes in which they both said things they later regretted.

"Yeah, right, so what do you think, that one day someone will discover you and we'll have our own little García Márquez writing his stupid junk about New York? I'd love to see you sell a book or two, maybe that's how we can get out of this goddamn toilet we live in."

"Why can't you just leave me alone, huh?"

"Instead of wasting your time with all those idiotic projects, why don't you find a woman of your own and get a life, get some kids of your own, a future, so that you don't get old and stay like this forever? You're really pathetic, you know that?"

"At least I give your children the warmth you don't give them. You don't pay them any attention, you never listen to them. For God's sake, I know your kids better than you do."

"Okay, why don't you go and get some kids of your own and leave mine in peace? Don't you bother them anymore or I'll get a restraining order to keep you away from them. I swear I'll do it."

She knew how to hit him where it hurt the most: her children, whom he adored and spoiled as if they were his own. He cherished his nephews and niece: he had been at their side when they were born and he had seen them learn how to talk, walk, read, and write. For him it was pure delight to watch Martín, Roberto, and Milagros grow up into mature human beings. He counseled them when they had trouble in school, regaled them with gifts, helped them out with their homework, and protected them whenever they sparked their mother's ire. Tío Fern always saved them from the slaps that, on certain occasions, their mother was all too ready to deliver. He knew that when they grew up they would remember him for the many times he interceded on their behalf, but for now they were still very young, and Patricia's control over their lives was ironclad. And she exercised this control even more once she finally achieved her objective, which was to win the lawsuit against the airline and keep the settlement for herself.

Ten years after the tragic accident, after countless presentations and meetings with the airline's lawyers, who came up with the most far-fetched conclusions—such as an airborne attack—to avoid conceding the company's responsibility in the plane crash, Fernando was disgusted with the entire process. He was all ready to wash his hands of the whole thing, but Patricia threatened to leave and take her children with her if he dropped the case.

At long last, a jury declared the airline responsible for the death of the seventy-three passengers who perished in the Avianca plane disaster, among them Doña Lucrecia. As such, the airline was ordered to pay $60,000 per victim, under the condition that the families would never file a countersuit or an appeal of any sort.

Patricia literally bubbled over with joy. Before the verdict, her voracious ambition and disdain for Fernando had never been a secret, but after the court decision was handed down, she launched an unthinkably devious plan that she had been hatching for a long time. Somehow, she had managed to fix things so that the money from the airline settlement went straight to her bank account. Fernando couldn't believe that she wasn't going to share it with the foundation he had established in Doña Lucrecia's name, the purpose of which was to continue the work she had always done for the underprivileged, and that she would have wanted them to continue, with abused children, immigrant women, and other at-risk groups. The foundation had been established to operate in both the United States and Colombia.

All of these causes, however, mattered very little to Patricia. And yet Fernando, little by little, began putting his own business aside and started dedicating more and more time to his mother's cause. In the neighborhood, people began to whisper that Fernando Travel was the place to go if you needed to resolve a tricky situation, and they all said that once someone sat on the other side of that sweet, friendly man's desk, he would help fix whatever problem came his way—as long, of course, as the problem wasn't illegal or harmful to another human being, the supreme creature for Fernando, the man who eventually became known as Don Fernando, the patron saint of the needy people of Jackson Heights.

All of this happened very slowly, as did the legal process that eventually culminated in his falling-out with Patricia. And it was during this period that Fernando decided to dedicate his energies toward the memory of his mother from the chair at the back of the office that, from the street outside, was known to all as Fernando Travel.

During that time he began to dream about his mother, picturing her as she chided him and urged him to do a better job fund-raising so that they could keep on doing what they were doing, taking care of those who died, alone and abandoned in New York, and sending them home to Colombia. Lots of times he didn't have enough money to buy a coffin. But then things would take a turn for the better. Like the day he received an unexpected call from a stranger who made the following offer:

"Fifteen top-quality coffins," the voice on the phone said. Fernando couldn't believe his ears. "I'm from Colombia, I manufacture luxury coffins. Business hasn't been very good, though, so I'm closing up shop. The thing is, I don't have anywhere to leave these coffins. Sending them back to Colombia is too expensive, so I'd rather donate them to you instead of taking them back home with me. People tell me that nobody in this town needs coffins like you do."

Fernando gratefully accepted the offer, and for several months a number of resplendent sarcophagi rested against the walls in his storefront, while others sat in Dr. Murtúa's office, like doors leading straight into heaven or hell. They inevitably caused a sensation when they arrived in Colombia, where the poor families couldn't believe that their loved ones had been granted eternal rest in such luxurious accommodations. On fifteen separate occasions, men and women who had been penniless on earth ended their days as ladies and gentlemen.

It wasn't until he tried to collect part of the settlement that Fernando discovered just how far his sister had gone. Silently, Patricia had created a legal structure designed to obstruct any effort her brother might make to collect his share of the money. She had declared herself the sole inheritor. That was how Fernando was summarily kicked out of the house he had purchased for his mother.

One day, in the middle of this battle, Patricia stomped into Fernando's room, grabbing papers, clothing, shoes, everything he owned, and threw it all out the window. The entire neighborhood witnessed the scene, and when it was over, Fernando disappeared for several days. The loss of his mother had been devastating enough, and this only made it worse. If his only sister, the sister he himself had helped raise, was capable of doing this, what on earth could he expect from anyone else?

He thought about his mother, and he felt sure that she was watching them from up above, feeling deeply ashamed about all that had transpired between them. And so, in addition to the family disaster and the deep sadness he felt, he was struck once again by an overwhelming sense of loneliness, like something that hung from his neck like a giant rock—a rock that he would have gladly taken with him into the sea, figuring that nobody would ever even realize he was gone.

• • •

Fernando picked his clothes off the ground as best he could, stuffing everything into the garbage bags that the children had brought him. They helped him as best they could, not fully understanding what it all meant. Of course, what it meant was that these bleak moments might very well be their last with Tío Fern. As they helped him gather his things, he tried to turn it all into a big game, to soften the blow, so that the children wouldn't take it so hard. When they were finished, he stroked their hair, kissed them on the forehead, and said,

"Go inside the house now. Now, I want you to forget about all this. This was all just a strange game that maybe, one day, I'll be able to explain to you."

Fernando started walking away with his two big garbage bags, not knowing where to go. He was totally alone now, and had nowhere to live. His sister had thrown him out of his own house, the house he himself had bought and put in his mother's name because, as he told his brothers and sister when he did it:

"I want our mother to know that she can do whatever she wants with this house because it is her property." For one last time he looked back at the home that he had bought and built with such great hope and sacrifice, in an attempt to achieve a dream, to unite a family. But to build a structure upon a false foundation, in this case to create a home with a group of people who didn't love each other . . . in the end perhaps he should have seen it coming. He was glad his mother hadn't been around to see it. At that moment he knew he would have to start from scratch, all over again, like any other recent arrival—except, of course, that now, so many years later, he knew so much more and had so much less energy. There he was, out on the street again, just like on his first day in the United States forty years earlier.

Out on the street, helpless, hopeless, and in despair, he took a deep breath and asked his mother to help him. To send him a message just to let him know that she had heard him. As he started walking, his feet took him to the safest place he knew: Fernando Travel. Patricia couldn't kick him out of there—if she could have, she already would have done so.

As he saw himself approach the front door, he finally cracked a smile, and he pulled out his keys, turned them in their locks, and went into the chilly storefront. Immediately, he turned on the heater, searched for the coffeepot, and put up some coffee. He was just about to pour himself a cup when he suddenly sensed that someone was watching him. Turning to look toward the door, he spied a tall, thin man peering inside insistently, tapping on the front door. Fernando walked over. As he opened it, the stranger said,

"Don Fernando, would you treat me to a cup of coffee?"

It was a voice that instantly brought him back to the coffee plantations of Armero, a voice from so many months earlier. Without missing a beat, Fernando said,

"Adrián, is that you?"

"Yes, sir, it's me. I was away in psychiatric treatment because I tried to kill myself. My ex-wife came to get me; she was the one who called 911 and saved me. But you've been on my mind, Fernando, because you have always been so generous with me. You treated me like a human being when I hit bottom. And I wanted to say thank you."

"You don't know how happy you've made me tonight, Adrián. And I have to say you've come at the most providential moment, like a message reminding me that not everything is lost, that as long as we're alive we have to keep on hoping, and acting with what we believe in our hearts. For me, at least, that is the real path that gives meaning to my life."

"Can I take you out to breakfast, Don Fernando?"

"I'm just brewing some coffee. In a little while we can call the luncheonette and ask them to bring us something to eat, what do you think?"

"That sounds good . . . Listen, a little later I want to call my ex-wife so that I can introduce her to you. I've told her all about you, and she'd like to meet you, maybe you can come over to dinner at our house one day."

"What's her name?"

"Lucrecia."

When he heard this, Fernando thought of his good mother and thanked her with all his heart. And then he poured two cups of sweet black coffee just the way they made it in his kitchen, at home when he was a little boy. In the home where he learned the importance of doing good things for people.

He smiled as he thought about her. After so many years it seemed that his mother still had a way of looking after him, sending him little messages so that he wouldn't give up his life's work. That was when the phone rang.

"Hello?"

At the other end, he heard a familiar voice that he didn't want to identify for fear that someone might be listening in on the conversation.

"I recognize you just fine, my friend. How are you and your wife?"

The voice, with a mix of Puerto Rican and Colombian inflections, announced the good news: his wife had just given birth to a little girl. They wanted Fernando to be the first to know, and they asked him to share the news with their good friends and of course the child's grandmother.

"What did you name her?" he said, and his eyes opened wide as he heard the name. "Just like my good mother! It will be my honor to be her godfather . . . Go? Of course I'll go! Just tell me where and when, and I'll be there. For now, I send you a big hug from here."

As soon as he hung up, he called his friends Murtúa and Sattui to invite them to a celebratory breakfast. But he waited until they were sitting down to eat to tell them the good news.

Acknowledgments

I wish to thank, first and foremost, my Latino community here in the United States. I am deeply grateful to the immigrants who struggle daily to achieve their dreams and some measure of happiness. Thanks to them, I have a reason to get up in the morning even when I am feeling defeated and battered by life's blows. They have shown me how to keep my faith and how to hold on to the hope for a new dawn, a new tomorrow.

I am very grateful to the entire group at Atria Books, especially Johanna Castillo, for her professional vision and faith in this project. I also offer my sincere thanks to Amy Tannenbaum, for always having a smile ready for me and for helping me with all the little questions, and to Judith Curr for publishing this book and opening the door to a new world. I would also like to thank the entire publicity department, and most especially my compatriot Melissa Quiñones for her joy and enthusiasm in promoting this book.

I also have a debt of gratitude to Joshua Marston, the director of the movie *Maria Full of Grace*, for reading and critiquing those stories in this book that are connected to his movie. For their editorial guidance, I would like to thank my friends Beto Ortiz and most especially Marcia Morgado, who was unflagging in her energy and unstinting in the love she lavished upon this project, working and re-working every last story. I would also like to thank my translator, Kristina Cordero, who worked with such magic and passion on this project.

Finally, I would like to thank God for giving me the health and the strength to make the dream of *Jackson Heights Chronicles* a reality.

About the Translator

Kristina Cordero is a translator of Spanish-language novels and nonfiction books. Her most recent translations include *Voyage Along the Horizon*, by Javier Marías, and *The Eagle's Throne*, by Carlos Fuentes. She is presently at work on a new translation, *The Essential Writings of St. Teresa of Ávila*.